# SPEAR OF DESTINY

---

## THE MISADVENTURES OF LOREN BOOK 1

### INES JOHNSON

THOSE JOHNSON GIRLS

# 1

 You can tell a lot about a man by the way he wields his sword.

 A man who jabs at his opponent's body with the tip of his blade using quick, jerky motions? That shows he's eager and unpracticed. If he gets in any good shots at all, they will likely be a hack job on his opponent's wrists and knuckles. That kind of action will leave him breathless and his opponent in need of a manicure. Also, he will probably never get asked to spar again after such an impotent showing.

 Then there are the ones who come at their opponent's body with a couple of long, deep thrusts. Those lunges might stem from a flexible groin and fluid wrist action, but that kind of foreplay can be misleading. These types of fighters often exert all their energy at the outset, relying solely on their strength and thrusting power. Then, after a moment of fighting, they roll over on their backs with exhaustion. Yeah, those swordsmen can simply have a seat. In fact, they can go and have several seats.

But the one who can hit all the targets by working his sword hand at just the right speed? The one who knows how to put pressure at just the right angle? The one who can use his blade to slice from the breast to the hip? Oh yeah, that type of swordsman can fill my dance card anytime.

Because that's what swordplay is: a dance. The movements more intimate than a waltz or a tango or whatever Baby and Johnny were doing up in the Catskills in the eighties with their bodies pressed together, their hips jamming to the music, and their legs and arms slicing into one another.

The opponent facing off against me was proving himself a worthy adversary and a superb dance partner. We faced each other with long swords, my weapon of choice. My stance was open at the moment as I prepared to go toe to toe with him. My weight was evenly balanced, my feet eager to advance. He held steady across from me, waiting to see what move I would make.

I took advantage of his courtesy and advanced. Leading with my left foot, I closed the distance between us. I stepped slightly to the right, to avoid any possible counterattack as I brought my blade straight down to his neck, going for the kill strike and preparing to slice his handsome head off from his lean body.

I feared I'd have to pull back at the last moment and not complete the advance, but he did not disappoint. He met my attack with a wrath strike, stepping off his line and bringing his blade down decisively against mine.

He had a good hundred pounds on me. But swordplay wasn't won with brute force alone. My thumb met my cross guard as my opponent tried to take control of the situation and pressure me off balance.

Silly boy.

I swiveled my wrist and thrust my sword, aiming for his heart. I knew by now that I didn't have to take it easy with him, and I was right. He stepped aside at the last minute and I met with air and empty space. I pivoted, sword raised, ready to advance again.

Wide grins slashed at the corners of both our faces. We both breathed hard from the exertion.

There was a hitch of desire to his deep voice as he spoke.

"Do you surrender, my lady?"

"No, sir. Not even when I'm handcuffed to a headboard."

That little remark caught him off guard, and I advanced.

The man I danced with was no English gentleman asking for my dance card. Nor was he an Argentinean count swiveling his hips in a tight pair of trousers and vest. And he absolutely wasn't some Jersey Boy with dirty moves beckoning me from the corner of a country club dinner table.

Sir Gawain, the third of his name, was a knight. One of King Arthur's knights. Yeah, that King Arthur. Though Arthur wasn't actually a king. Just another thing that history got wrong. But Arthur did have a castle, complete with a round table and magical swords. Gawain and I were training in the backyard of said castle on the grounds of Camelot.

The clanging of sharp metal brought me back to the present and out of my musings about male dancers and castles and swords. Overhead, the grumble of a passenger plane punctuated the clash of swords. Someone's cellphone played the theme to *Final Fantasy*, providing a soundtrack to the battle.

Gawain came at me with an overhaul strike. He brought his sword down against mine, hard. My lower body wasn't braced, and the blow reverberated down to my knees rendering me to the ground.

Gawain pulled his blade back at the last second so it didn't pierce my boobs. But the retraction cost him his balance. He tumbled to the ground on top of me and my boobs, which were covered in chain mail for my protection. Another pity since my boobs were my most fearsome weapons.

"Are you alright, Lady Loren?" Gawain asked as he loomed above me.

His dark curtain of hair brushed each of my cheeks. His angled eyes were a deep coffee brown and not black like I had originally thought. His nose was a long slope that curved at the tip. A lush forest of hair outlined the skin above his upper lip and entirely covered his chin.

This man, this dark knight, was all svelte muscle. From this angle, I caught a glimpse inside his linen shirt and was rewarded with a view of the defined chest I had yet to taste. But my gaze fixed on his mouth and the name he'd called me.

I'd been called a lot of things in my life. Beautiful. Thief. Fashionable. Liar. All true. But I'd never been called a Lady, like, as a title of honor. Because for a long time, I didn't have any honor.

I was a woman with all the requisite parts including long legs that could rock a six-inch pair of heels. A trim waist that looked best in a halter dress or wrap skirt. My long blonde hair was all my own, no weave or extensions, which meant it was perfect for a man to gather in his fist and tug if the mood was right. And man, oh man, was I in the right mood for this shining knight. No armor necessary.

"You nearly had me," said Gawain as he stood and offered me his forearm to give me a lift up. "If only you'd stepped off your center line, you could've evaded my blade."

I hadn't done anything wrong. I had the knight right where I wanted him. I reached for his forearm and gave a tug before he could brace himself to hoist me up. Gawain lost his footing and came down on top of me again.

"Oops," I said as two-hundred twenty pounds of virile man came crashing down on my welcome body. This time, his nose met with the valley of my breasts. Like I said, I hadn't done anything wrong.

Gawain braced himself so that his forearms took the brunt of his weight and not my boobs. Pity.

A grin lit his wicked lips as his brown eyes twinkled. "Why do I get the feeling I'm the one who's fallen into the trap?"

"'Cause you've got brain and brawn." I slid one leg up, bending at the knee to trap him further. "Wanna show me again how to properly thrust a sword? I'm sure I'll get it this time if I concentrate real hard."

Gawain chuckled and made no move to escape, until a voice sounded over us.

"I told you this was a waste of time."

I'd completely forgotten that we had an audience. Looking to the side, I took a moment to admire the eye candy all around me. From my position down low, I panned and tilted my gaze around the long feet, thick thighs, and bulging chests of the men assembled. Yum-oh.

For a century, photographic, motion film, and television cameras had been capturing images. For most of that time, men had been training the lenses on women's body parts; the Male Gaze it was called. Cameramen zoomed unapologetically onto our boobs and asses. They panned up our legs and tilted up our skirts to display our wares on the big screen. So, I had no trouble turning the tables on them from my low vantage point.

Gawain ended my screening early. He rose to his

feet, pulling me up alongside him with strong arms. His action brought me face to face with my complainer.

"She'll never take her place amongst us as a knight," said Sir Geraint.

Geraint's eyebrows were set in a perpetual arch, like the symbol used to accent letters. It made every statement he said in his droll voice seem incredibly dramatic. Even though I had yet to see him smile or laugh or speak in anything other than a tone brimming with disdain.

Like the other five knights present, Geraint had long, lush locks, and a face covered by a thick beard. Beneath his dark hair, the mocha skin of his Moorish ancestry shone through. Another thing the story books got wrong. The knights of Camelot were a diverse bunch. From Gawain and his Asian heritage, to Percival and his Middle Eastern birthright, all the way to Lance with his Highland ginger looks, and back around to the youngest knight, Tristan, with his angelic face and blond, Icelandic legacy.

And then there was the man himself, Arthur.

Although I'd learned that that wasn't really his name. All of these men were descendants of the original Knights of the Roundtable. When they succeeded their fathers, they took on the title. That meant each knight was *The* Arthur and *The* Lancelot.

I was the granddaughter of Sir Galahad, the second of his name. But granddad had left no sons. His two daughters, my mother and my aunt, each had girls. The seat of Galahad had been empty for over three hundred years. But the sword of Galahad had found its way to me outside of this magical place.

I hadn't known about this side of my family. My mother had run away from this place to be with my dad—an archaeologist. After I was born, we'd traveled the world with him. Every night as a child, my mother read me stories about Arthur and his knights, about Camelot and quests, and wizards and witches. But she never told me that any of the tales were real. She never told me I was a part of these books that I loved.

But like I said, I'd found my way here. And now I was ready to claim my rightful place: a seat at the freaking Round Table. If I could just get past all this chivalry and chauvinism crap.

Arthur stepped forward. He looked the spitting image of Liam Hemsworth with his dirty blond hair and light gray eyes. His huge biceps were crossed over his massive chest as he pinned me with his assessing gaze like a headmaster. I should mention, I got kicked out of boarding school when I was a teen in a blaze of glory.

"Geraint's right," Arthur said.

My head snapped up, way up, and I suddenly felt three feet tall. I couldn't be sure, but I think my bottom lip may have trembled as I asked, "What?"

"This was a mistake."

"Oh, come on, Artie."

The Arthur glared down, shaving off another foot of my bravado.

I'd been in life or death situations. I'd even died once—another story. But Arthur was the only man who made me squirm and not in the good way. He didn't know me very well. So, he didn't know that I used humor and sass when I felt intimidated.

"My liege." I executed a bow I'd seen on one of the BBC historical programs. "I'm just getting started with my training. At least give me a chance to actually screw up."

"That's my point," said Arthur. "You're just getting started. Every knight trains from birth to take his seat. We all start out as a page, learning our duties. Then after a few decades, we advance to a squire."

Geraint came up beside Arthur, rubbing his

hairy chin. The arches of his brows rose as the hint of a smile touched the corner of his mouth. "Making her a squire isn't a bad idea."

"Okay," I said. "What's a squire have to do?"

From the corner of my eye, I saw Gawain wince. Percival's lips quirked up and his eyes twinkled as though he were expecting rousing entertainment. Tristan shut his eyes and bit his lip as though he were anticipating his parents starting an argument.

"A squire is... let's see if I can find a human term..." Geraint continued to toy with his whiskers.

I let the *human* crack slide, but not too far. I'd spent a good deal of my life defending my human father and his reputation. But that had been against other humans who'd disdained his research methods. Now I'd have to take it from magical kind? Because knights were magical. They had a special sauce running through their blood that enhanced their strength and allowed them to live long lives.

"Humans might call a squire an apprentice," Geraint continued. "They tend to a knight's weapons and his horse. They care for our personal effects. And do odd jobs around the castle."

I cocked my head to the side as I glared at his pointy brows. "You want me to be an errand boy?"

Geraint grinned for the first time since I'd met

him. "I believe the politically correct term is personal assistant."

I rolled my head around, hearing the tendons in my neck crack along the way. Oh. No. He. Didn't. "You want me to be a secretary?"

He shrugged. "If the armor doesn't fit."

I dropped the practice sword and picked up my grandfather's sword, the magical sword of Galahad. I pointed to the sword holstered at Geraint's side. "Draw your sword."

"What?" Geraint held up his hands. "I don't fight girls."

"I'm not a girl."

I charged. Geraint gripped his weapon with both hands a split second before I brought the wrath down upon him.

"I am a grown ass woman who was trained by the best swordsmen over the world since I was nine."

I had been holding back with Gawain, toying with him because I wanted to dance with him in more ways than one. Facing Geraint, I wasn't playing footsie anymore.

"I have gold medals in swordplay," I said. "Not a single one that's silver or bronze or for participation."

Geraint jabbed at me with quick, jerky thrusts. I

wasn't the least bit surprised at his sloppy swordplay. I unloaded on him. Swiveling my sword, I made figure eights around my body as I advanced on him.

I double fisted my sword, aiming for his throat. He dodged and took a deep lunge into me, thrusting with his sword arm. I parried his single-handed blow, hard enough to disarm him. Then I thrust the hilt of my sword backward and into his chest. He went down with an *oomph*. I came over top of him with my blade pointed at that arch in his brows. My hands were on fire as I advanced on him.

"And if you ever call me a secretary again, I'll cut off your eyebrows."

The hilt of my sword was in flames. Literally. Fire licked at the leather bindings and then down to the wooden part of the cane. I dropped the burning sword and shook my flaming hands, trying to douse the flare of magic.

Oh, did I forget to mention that my mother was a witch, and I'd recently come into my powers? I'll come back to that. First, I needed to get my powers under control.

I clenched my fists tightly. After a couple of deep breaths, my hands cooled. But not my temper.

"Like I said," Geraint uttered from his place on the ground. "She's untrained and out of control, a liability if we take her into the field. And we don't even know if she can be trusted. Her mother stole that sword and her father is a notorious fraud in the human world. Someone like her can't take Sir Galahad's seat."

I felt my hands heating up again, but I balled my fists even tighter. Half my life I'd spent under the cloud of insults against my father and his work, when my father had been innocent of the crime he was accused of.

Well.

Kind of.

Mostly.

People just needed to know the whole story to understand. But no one ever listened. They all just labeled him a villain and moved on. I'd been cast under the same label back in the human world and it would appear I wouldn't escape it here in the magical town of Camelot.

The fire had gone out of my hands and my spirit. Looking down, I saw that the wood of the cane that had hidden the magical sword of my grandfather had burned away. The cane had been my father's.

All that was left was the blade. The steel winked at me under the sunlight. I leaned down to pick it up.

"Where did you learn that?" Arthur asked.

"Gwin's been trying to teach me to control the magic. It's just that it's so much—"

"Not the magic. The swordplay."

"Oh." I blinked as I looked up at him. "I've been taking fencing lessons since I could walk." I'd learned from the world's greatest masters, including a certain Spartan King forever immortalized in a Hollywood film, King Leonidas. But that's yet another story. "I've been felling men twice my size since I was twelve."

Arthur studied me anew. I held still, realizing for the first time exactly how much I wanted his approval. That scared me more than the magic rushing through my blood. Waiting for his judgment felt like my skin was being sheared off my bones.

"I'm not gonna jump through your hoops," I said. "I'll just take my sword and go."

"You can't leave," said Arthur. "Not with a power you can't control coursing through your veins. You need protection more than you need training."

"I'm no man's damsel."

"The truth is, Loren, you're not giving us a chance. You need training—as a witch in addition to a knight. But even before that, you need to earn the respect of the men here if you want to be accepted into our ranks."

There was that word again. Acceptance. Did I want their acceptance?

"You're a part of this family," said Arthur. "You belong here with us."

My arms instinctively wrapped around my middle. Though my parents were both gone, I did have other family, my father's family. But they'd rejected me when I was a little kid. Right after I'd lost my mother. And then again after I lost my father. I'd never expected to hear those words again: *you have family, you belong.* And Arthur wasn't done.

"The sword chose you to wield it, but the knights choose who takes a seat at the Round Table."

"So you want me to be your little gopher?" I hadn't signed up to be in the shadows. I'd spent half my life cast as a femme fatale, a role which, admittedly, I'd cultivated and had the wardrobe and smoky voice to support. But I was done being the villain or the sidekick. I was ready to be the hero of the story.

"We all had to squire before we earned our seat," said Arthur. "If you want to be treated like an equal amongst the knights, if you want to earn your grandfather's seat, then you'll need to earn our respect."

I looked around at the bearded faces assessing

me. My gaze stuck on Gawain and his sultry eyes. And then I realized, these knights were all men. I could have each of them wrapped around my finger before the week was out.

"Fine," I said. "Hit me with it. I can handle whatever you throw at me."

Yeah, right. Two cliché catch phrases in a row? I was clearly asking for trouble.

2

---

"These need to be cleaned and polished," said the young man before me.

My knees buckled as a literal ton of dull metal was piled into my arms. After much debate, where Geraint suggested I be a Chamber Squire and put on a housekeeping detail and it took Lance and Gawain to hold me back from cleaning his clock, it was decided I'd be put in the armory.

The weapons room inside the castle was a mix of medieval weaponry and modern technology. Steel blades, chains, and shields covered the wall of one corner, while guns of every shape and size were arrayed on another. In the farthest corner, computers and electronic gadgets buzzed and beeped. In a third corner were weights, punching bags, and sparring dummies. It looked like the knights had covered all the bases of medieval, modern, and high-tech warfare.

Inside the armory with me were three other squires on weapons detail this morning. There was the curly headed Yuric who was so thin he looked like the wind would knock him over. And then there was Maurice who looked like a mountain. The pair reminded me of the nursery rhyme of non-fat eating Jack Sprat and his portly wife who ate no lean.

And then there was Baysle, the squire who'd handed me the pile of weaponry. Not basil, a favorite herb of mine and the best part of a true Italian Margherita pizza. The word basil was said with a soft-sounding 'A' that ended lightly on the final consonant. The way Baysle said his name when he introduced himself it sounded like he was vomiting out the *Ba* sound and then choking on the ending consonant; Bah-*Zil*.

The kid was handsome. But he was the kind who knew it. I pinched my nose at the airs he put on.

Baysle wore the seal of Sir Geraint, letting me know he was the knight's personal squire. Which by default made him a douche-in-training. He squinted his green eyes at me. Angling his body away, he took a second glance at the priceless bounty in my arms and then squinted back up at me.

"Best to stay inside the armory while you get those done," he said.

The kid was lucky my arms were full of swords so I couldn't reach out and wring his neck. But then again, my arms were full of swords. I could drop all but one and slice the pipsqueak in half.

I didn't miss the judgment in his assessing gaze. Nor his conclusion about my morals. Early in life, I'd been cast as a villain. The role had been thrust upon me by a number of circumstances. None of them I'd actually auditioned for, mind you.

It started before I was born. My mother had run away from home to be with my dad. When she did, she took something with her from her family. It was an heirloom passed down from father to son. But by the time she'd been born, there had been no more sons born along her family line. Only daughters.

Anyway, the item my mom had taken had been the sword of her grandfather, Sir Galahad, first of his name. I hadn't known I'd been wielding a magical sword in the skirmishes I'd been getting into all my life. I'd simply thought I was a bad ass. And I was.

The sword hadn't taught me my awesomeness. I'd learned those lessons on my own. The sword had enhanced what was already there.

I'd brought the sword back a quarter century later, not knowing what it was until I'd dropped it in the moat in front of the castle. The Lady of the Lake had emerged and handed the sword back to me, proclaiming me as its rightful owner like another royal orphan. Prophetic, I know.

But still, I was watched as I walked through these halls. I knew the gazes upon me looked at me as someone who might steal. It didn't help that I'd come to these halls as the guest of someone who had stolen from these people in the past.

My bestie, Nia, had brought me here weeks ago. She was the Wonder Woman of history, rescuing ancient sites and artifacts from zealous developers and tomb raiders. I'd tagged along as her sidekick when she came to help the knights out on their last quest. Nia admittedly had grabby hands for ancient things and we'd both gotten antique boners when we'd been let inside the medieval castle.

Speaking of bones, that's how she and I met.

When I was still a girl, my dad had told a necessary lie based on an unbelievable truth. It had cost him his reputation, his livelihood, and perhaps even his life. Nia had helped me to unravel the mess that my dad had made and restore the Van Alst family name. But those in the antiquities world still looked at me with a squint in their eyes when they heard my last name.

For a time, when I'd been on my own, I'd worn that bad girl label like a badge of honor and I was good at it. Being the daughter of an archaeologist, my fingers were a bit sticky when it came to prized artifacts. I'd been known to raid a tomb or two in my past. I also had an eye for art and could easily copy just about any painting I saw and pass it off as the real deal.

But that was all backstory. That life was so six months ago. Wow. Had it been that long? I'd met my best friend, upgraded from villain to a heroine's sidekick, and learned I was a witch. Now, if I could just get past these stupid trials, I'd earn my stripes as a bona fide hero and take a seat as a knight at the Round Table.

So, I'd put up with *Bah-zil*, the twerp's, abuse. For now.

Baysle went to the opposite side of the room where the electronic gadgets, computers, and modems, and tablets were kept. He sat down behind one such console. His head disappeared, and I heard the unmistakable tone of an Xbox being powered on.

I looked over at the other two boys around me. They ignored Baysle and got to work on their duties. These boys were all in their teens, though they had been on the earth before I was born. Sure, they looked like teenagers with the beginnings of facial hair and limbs still being grown into. But each of these guys was at least twice my age in actual years.

Time moved differently in Camelot. Or rather, it moved the same, but with the magic flowing through the veins of the people of this small town, time had little effect on them. As long as the witches, wizards, and warriors stayed on the ley line that ran beneath the surface they stayed youthful, moving slowly through life. If they were off the ley line for too long, the absence of the magic allowed their natural age to catch up with them. And then there would be a whole reverse Benjamin Button on their hands.

"Here," said Maurice, "I'll take those.

The big guy reached for my load of swords. I was surprised to hear such a gentle voice come out of such a large male. I let him take the swords and bent to pick up a cleaning rag, but Yuric got to the cloth before I did.

"This isn't women's work, my lady," Yuric said.

My hackles went up. But not so far. They were doing my chores for me. It appeared boys did a lot of chores around the town and castle. Little pages cleaned while Gwin directed the workings as the Lady of the Castle. The matronly Igraine cooked all the meals but the pages, again all boys, served the dishes during mealtimes. Around the town, most of the shops were owned and operated by women and staffed by young girls.

I'd fallen into some feminist's wet dream. But there was a problem.

"I'm a squire," I said, "not a lady."

I took the rag back and a couple of the swords. I plopped myself down in a chair and got to work. This was actually work I enjoyed, cleaning and sharpening a fine blade.

Above me, Yuric and Maurice looked at each other. They were Lance and Arthur's squires, two of the most chivalrous knights in the castle. The boys were likely trying to decide how much trouble they'd get into for letting a woman do man's work.

"What are we polishing these for anyway?" I asked. "Are we going to use them in battle?"

"Squires don't fight," said Yuric. "We don't even leave Camelot much. Not since Merlin... well, you know."

Since Merlin had tried to take Gwin's magic and leave the knights to their greatest enemies, the Knights Templars? Yeah, I did know. I'd had a front row seat to that bit of action.

Merlin, Arthur's older brother, hadn't exactly been the great wizard recorded in the storybooks. He'd been born with magic. But that magic had nearly killed him.

There were many witches born, but very few wizards. Most boys were born to be knights with just enough magic that they became strong warriors, able to wield magical swords and handle magical artifacts and defend against magical adversaries. When a boy was born with too much magic, the power could render his body weak and leave him ill or even dead.

That's what happened to Merlin. So, what did he do about it? He acted like a little punk. Throughout his marriage, he siphoned off his wife's magic to keep him strong and alive.

Merlin's wife was Gwin. Yup, that Guinevere. And apparently, she wasn't enough for him because he took his magic-grubbing hands outside his marriage and went homicidal.

Merlin had taken the magic of some of the witches living outside of Camelot. But by this time he'd stopped sipping and took deep gulps of their magic which left them for dead. The knights had believed the culprits to be their sworn enemies, the Knights Templars. Imagine their shock when they found out it was the heir to the throne. And worse, he was still on the loose today. Which made the knights even more protective than normal.

"We train and we do our duties until we're old enough to take our places as knights," Yuric was saying.

"Sounds boring." I laid down a polished broadsword and picked up a sai. "I usually get into trouble when I get bored."

"We have a lot of duties," said Maurice. "The knights give us more than enough to keep us occupied."

"Who is Sir Gawain's squire?" I asked. If I got to clean his personal weapons that might make this whole squire-hazing a bit more palatable.

Because it was hazing. I had all the qualifications of being a knight, except my sword was on my hip instead of between my legs.

I looked up when the silence stretched on a bit long. The two boys looked at each other.

"Sir Gawain doesn't have any pages or a squire," said Yuric. "He used to. But then he faced the Green Knight."

I snorted as I wiped my rag over the sai's flat side. "That's not real. It's just a-"

"Story?" said Yuric. "Then we're all stories, my lady."

I knew the stories about Gawain and the Green Knight. The storybooks told that the knight had faced a powerful warrior that was death incarnate. But that hadn't actually happened in real life. Had it? It would mean that Death was a person.

But then again, I had met Zeus and his brother Hades a couple of months ago. I'd once thought that the tales of the Olympians had been just stories. And my best friend was an Immortal being who was thousands of years old and nearly impenetrable to disease and decay. And I could now shoot fire out of my hands.

I'd seen some crazy, magical things happen this year. Like flying ninjas who drank bones. Greek gods who sucked out people's souls. I'd watched a woman come back from the dead after having an ancient witch's magic transferred to her body.

Oh wait, that was me. But I was hoping to draw the line at death having an appointment with the guy I had the hots for.

"Magical swords," said Yuric. "A lady in the lake. An enchanted castle. A knight from the line of Galahad who retrieves the Holy Grail for Arthur."

Yeah, all those stories were now facts I'd witnessed and taken part in. Technically, I was the Grail now. The actual Holy Grail hadn't been a cup. It had been Mary Magdalene who, it turns out, was a witch. She was also Arthur's ancestor. Mary's husband, Joseph of Arimathea, had bucked tradition and hadn't burn his wife's body as was the custom with witches. Instead, he entombed it. If a witch's body wasn't burned the magic stayed alive in her corpse. To keep the magic from the bad guys, Mary Magdalene's powers had been transferred into me as I'd lay dying from a bad guy's knife to my chest.

"But all the stories can't be real," I said. "Like Sir Bors' tale? After taking a vow of celibacy, he supposedly had a lady and her maidens threaten to throw themselves off the castle battlements. When he refuses, they do jump and reveal themselves to be demons sent to tempt him."

"That was real, my lady," said Maurice. "God rest Lady Evie's soul."

I looked between the two of them. Neither laughed like it was a joke. "Okay, okay. What about Percival? Was he raised in a forest by his mother?"

"Not exactly," said Yuric. "He was raised in captivity, but not in a forest."

That kind of made sense. Where Geraint's brow was arched in an accent, Percy's brows reminded me of the top of an exclamation point. I expected him to shout *bang* or *boogedyboo* at any and every moment. He looked as though he was feral and had a few screws loose.

The knights' tales from the stories were a soap opera of adultery and betrayal and murder and bedhopping and *You killed my father, prepare to die.* I knew all the tales because my mom read them to me as a little girl. She just didn't tell me any were true. But here I was living in the fantasy world in the twenty-first century.

"We need to hurry up and finish," said Baysle as he powered down the Xbox. "It's nearing lunchtime."

"We?" I demanded.

"Yeah," said Baysle. "We're a team. I'm the leader. Chop, chop." He made a brushing motion with his empty hands. And with that, he headed out the room.

"Ignore him," said Yuric. "He got his head stuck in a helmet when he was younger."

"They still haven't gotten it off yet?" I asked.

Both Maurice and Yuric laughed. I had a couple choicer words about Baysle, but I held my tongue. No sense corrupting the youth the first day on the job. We had time.

"I think it's good that the knights are integrating," said Yuric. "Lady Morgan says that too many men are trapped in a single sense of masculinity that reinforces patriarchy and male privilege."

"Yuric?" I asked. "Do you understand any of what you just said?"

"No, he doesn't," said Maurice. "He was too busy watching Lady Morgan's lips as she said the words."

Yuric reached over and punched Maurice, but it barely made an impact on the big guy.

"I don't believe that the genders are equal." Maurice shrugged his shoulders apologetically. "There are things that women can do that men can't. There are also tasks that women can do that a man should be tarred and feathered if he doesn't take upon himself to do. But I don't think that makes either sex inferior. I'm glad you're here, Lady Lo."

"Wow." I sniffed, dramatically. "Thanks guys."

"All right," said Maurice. "That's enough

menstruating. Let's get these weapons put up and get some grub."

Look at that. It was only my first day at knight school and I was making friends. Which was a world different than when I'd gone to actual school. Score a point for me.

## 3

With our duties done, I went with the other squires to put my swords up. A few other squires I didn't know very well came to the door and called to Yuric and Maurice, inviting them to lunch. It didn't surprise me that I'd fallen in with the guys. I'd never been the type to have girlfriends. Likely because women found me intimidating. But I could always pal around with the boys. I was excited to meet some more of my fellow squires.

I placed the last sword on the rack and grabbed my satchel. When I turned back around, the room was silent and empty. The door was shut and they were all gone. They'd left me behind.

I could've called out to them, but a thickness settled in my throat. My shoulders slumped, likely from the heavy weights of the swords I'd been carrying. I wrapped my arms around myself to alleviate some of the tension as I headed towards the door.

Maybe it had been a mistake? Maybe they expected I was behind them? I walked out the armory door to see the group walking down the hall, shoulder to shoulder. They poked fun at each other and laughed their jabs off. No one looked back to see if I was there. And so, I kept my distance.

The simple truth was I hadn't honed my skills with boys until I was older. So, young boys weren't exactly in my wheelhouse. Grown men, however? I usually had them eating out of my hands.

As we passed by the Throne Room where the Round Table was housed, I heard low voices. I peered across the threshold of the room to see that the knights were in deep conversation. Everyone's eyes were intent on the speaker, listening hard.

Gawain caught my eye and smiled. Then my view was blocked. Geraint sneered as he swaggered towards the great door and then he shut it in my face.

So okay, I'd never been the type to fit in with a large group of males. One on one was better. I'd had a string of lovers, but since I was a bit allergic to commitment, they never stuck around. Much like my father's family.

I carried the name Van Alst and had a small trust fund that they'd tried unsuccessfully to keep away from me. When my father delivered me to their doorstep when he'd had to go on a particularly rough dig, they'd shoved me into a boarding school after only two weeks of knowing me. It took me a couple of months to get kicked out and for my father to come get me. I never left his side again, until he died.

I looked around the hallways of the castle, wondering which way to turn. I decided to head into the kitchen to find Igraine, the closest thing I'd ever had to a grandmother. But when I got there, Igraine was nowhere to be found. She was likely in the Great Hall eating with the rest of the community.

But the kitchens weren't empty. Morgan and Gwin were standing over the stove. In the original Arthur stories, Morgan Le Faye was Arthur's sorceress sister that he'd had an illicit affair with. Guinevere was his wife who had an adulterous affair with his best knight, Lancelot.

That was not this story.

Morgan and Gwin were sisters. Morgan had dark hair, an argumentative wit, and an anarchist attitude.

Gwin was blonde and proper and perfect. And I was their black sheep of a cousin.

They were older than me by a handful of decades, but physically, we looked like contemporaries. Their parents had retired and were living in Florida. Apparently, there was a ley line near Walt Disney World. So, the three of us were the last of the line of Sir Galahad, with Gwin being the oldest and me bringing up the rear.

The sisters stood in a tight huddle as they peered into a pot. The ladle went around the edges of the cauldron of its own accord. With one hand, Morgan tossed in dried plants. With another, she tossed in pulverized herbs.

"A little essential oil for the soul. Alcohol for the spirit." Morgan opened her hand and a bottle of wine floated into her grasp. She opened the spirits and dashed in a splash. Then she grabbed a pinch from a salt dish. "And salt for the body."

"I don't think it'll work," said Gwin. "Science and magic don't often coexist well."

"Science and magic together are what makes alchemy," said Morgan. "They work perfectly together under the right hand."

Morgan mumbled a few words that I couldn't hear. In the few magic lessons I'd had, Gwin had told me that the words didn't matter. The chant just helped a witch to focus her powers, much like the *Om* of meditation.

Whatever Morgan chanted sounded like a calming hum. The brew bubbled up. Its rapid growth appeared to rattle the sides of the cauldron making the kettle shake on the stove grate. A green foam grew into a volcano and then the top popped in a loud burst. Goo splattered with a wet plop on both of the sister's noses.

"Morgan," Gwin groaned, looking down at her shirt. "This is my favorite top."

Morgan scooped a dollop of goo from her lower eyelid. "I must have added a little too much alcohol."

Gwin turned to her sister, her face indignant. Morgan wore a frown of disappointment as she turned her gaze from the pot to look at her sister. The two faced each other in silence as they surveyed the damage done.

Morgan's finger crooked at her sister's top and she snorted. Gwin swiped away the green brew from her sister's cheek with a giggle. Beside them, the cauldron burped and the sisters laughed hysterically.

I watched them for a moment as they wiped themselves off. I'd been an only child. I didn't quite understand how siblings could go from angry with each other one second to the best of friends the next. It looked nice. I scratched at my chest, turning on my heel.

"Loren," called Morgan. "Hey, where are you going?"

"Oh," I said turning back. "I was just... I was going..."

I had nowhere to be, no one to go with, no one waiting for me.

"See," said Morgan looking at me and motioning to the bubbling brew. "This wouldn't happen if I was working in an actual lab instead of in a thirteenth-century kitchen."

"We remodeled in the twentieth," said Gwin, looking around at the stainless steel appliances on the other side of the room which barely got used by the old school witches who cooked in the kitchens.

"God, I need to get out of this place," said Morgan. "I'm going to go crazy here."

"You're being dramatic, Morgan," said Gwin as she set about cleaning up the mess that Morgan had just made. "You have enough to do with your duties here and your academic studies."

"Yeah, at my online university," Morgan grumbled. "Chemistry should be done in a laboratory with beakers and Bunsen burners, not a crockpot."

With the looming threat of his brother out in the real world, Arthur had decreed that all witches stay on the grounds of Camelot, which grounded Morgan who'd been accepted into Cambridge's graduate program.

Morgan turned her navy-blue gaze on me. Mischief I'd only ever seen in a bathroom mirror twinkled at me. "You think if I blew something up The Arthur would finally be pissed enough to release me from this prison?"

I wasn't sure whether to laugh or to draw up a list of explosive materials to gather.

Gwin rolled her eyes as she looked away from her sister and at me. "You have lunch yet, Loren?"

"Um, well..." I started.

"You'll come with us," said Morgan.

They came toward me, walking shoulder to shoulder. Then they opened their circle and beckoned me into it. I slipped between the two sisters and we headed out of the kitchen and out of the castle through a back door.

"Speaking of school," said Gwin. "Are you ready for your next lesson?"

Gwin was trying to teach me to control my

powers. She was a great teacher. I'd just been a horrible student all of my life, much preferring to learn from the school of hard knocks than an actual instructor. But there were no YouTube videos on how to be a witch. So, I had to listen.

So far I'd learned to shoot fire out of my hands, and I wasn't very good at that. I wasn't ready for another lesson. Not after the morning I'd had.

"I'm a bit tuckered out from knight training. Or should I say squire training."

"What?" Morgan gasped. Her ears went red, and her face screwed in indignation. "They demoted you to squire? They're all a bunch of pigs. You know what this calls for? A little retail therapy. I happen to have access to Arthur's accounts."

"Oh," I sighed, my heart melting at her devious plan. "We are so related."

"Morgan," said Gwin in a warning tone. "We can't use those accounts unless it's for the castle."

Morgan and I looked at each other. Then we each looped an arm around through Gwin's and tugged her out across the bridge and into town.

It didn't take much convincing to lure Gwin to the dress shop, especially when we pointed out the damage done on the job to her favorite top. We had a delightful conversation about worker's compensation on the way. Gwin was a goody two shoes witch, but she was also a warm-blooded female.

We walked against the flow as the townsfolk headed into the castle for the midday meal. Most of the work stopped for about an hour like a Southern Spanish town on siesta while people left the rat race and broke bread with their neighbors.

Elderly knights made their way toward the castle dressed in slacks and kirtles. Some witches were dressed in tunic dresses and surcoats that trailed to the ground. Others wore jeans and peasant blouses with pointy-toed shoes. The teens wore a mix of fashions with boys in leather pants and boots to gym shorts and girls in mini-skirts and laced bodices.

Modern and medieval lived harmoniously in this small corner of the world. The magical town of Camelot was situated in the modern-day town of Caerleon in Wales. The majority of the residents were magic kind, but human tourists mingled in with the locals on the weekends, oblivious to the supernatural in the medieval-themed town.

But not today. Today was Tuesday, a notoriously slow day for tourists. The fake sword in the stone exhibit sat abandoned with no fanny-pack toting parents forcing their kids to take a staged photo. No one stood reading the placards of an embellished history of the legend of the great Arthur's place in Caerleon.

The placards made up lies from the truth. The words etched in stone told of a battle the great Arthur fought in Caerleon, the City of the Legion. According to legend, as written by Geoffrey Monmouth, Arthur held court for the feast of Whitsuntide here in Caerleon. He called forth his chieftain allies to sail down the River Usk to join him and renew their pacts of peace.

It was a great story. It just never happened here. The current Arthur was the third of his name. It had happened with his great-grandfather, Arthur the first, son of Uther Pendragon. And it had taken place back in Glastonbury, the original home of Camelot.

But the stone gimmick, and the placard marking the feast, along with a few other carefully crafted tales kept the truth hidden from humans. Hiding in plain sight they called it. That and the protective charm placed around the castle.

As I stepped away from the castle and onto the path into the city, I felt a marked change in the atmosphere. I hadn't felt it before, when I was more human than witch. But stepping away from the castle and the protective charm today was like shedding an outer coat. I shivered as we continued down the road.

We were greeted by all as we weaved through. People didn't just say hello to Morgan and Gwin. They spoke to me as well. And not just cordial niceties.

They asked how I was settling in. They asked if I needed anything. They made me promise to come by and see them for a cup of tea, to deliver a keepsake that they had of my mother's, or just to spend a little time.

The chill that had settled on my shoulders lifted as we came out the other side of the crowd. Standing between Gwin and Morgan as they chattered on, I felt like I was in a cocoon. Or no, a nest with the bum of a big bird keeping me warm until I was ready to fly.

It may sound corny, and a little gross. But it felt nice. Being a part of something, being included, being accepted, felt nice. Which made me wonder just how long would it last?

## 4

_____

We crossed the cobblestone street and headed for Minerva's Modern Medieval Market, a mouthful if you dared to mumble it. Minerva was coming out of the storefront door and turning the lock when we stepped onto the sidewalk.

"You're eating out today?" asked Morgan. Her sultry voice hit the high-pitched whine of a child.

"Just up to the castle," Minerva smiled at the three of us. "Worked my fingers to the bone on a new corset. Decided to give them a break and my belly a treat and see what Igraine was serving today."

Minerva was tall with an hourglass shape. Like most women in the town, she wore a mashup of time periods. Her simple, wrap skirt could've come down the runway of Italy. The waist was cinched with leather bindings. Mounted on her shoulders were golden epaulets. Her hair was done up in intricate braids like a crown. On her feet, she wore a nude shoe, but the underbelly was the unmistakable red calling card of Louboutins.

Now I understood Morgan's whine. If this was Minerva's everyday wear, I was itching to see what she created for her customers. Clothes and fashion were my weakness. I typically went for the high-end, straight off the runway, and designer labeled articles. But once the wares were in my closet, I loved to mix and match, especially the vintage with the contemporary.

"Did you and the Arthur have one of your rows?" asked Minerva eyeing Morgan. Before Morgan could respond, Minerva turned the lock from closed to open. "You ladies go in and do as much damage as you please. I'll put it on his accounts."

Minerva winked at us as she headed down the street towards the castle. I turned from her and walked into the shop. The moment my feet crossed the threshold, my mouth was salivating.

There was a rack of tunic dresses. They ventured from the long and fitted to accent the figure, to the short and loose to reveal the figure. There were fur-trimmed gowns made of velvet. Lace-trimmed gowns made of satin. Prim wimples and elaborate headdresses shaped like hearts and butterflies. I loved headdresses. The only reason I ever considered getting married, or going to church, was so that I could wear one.

But it just wasn't the medieval styles on display. Minerva also had the latest fashions of the day. There were designer jeans, leather jackets, crew neck shirts. There were even those godawful shirts with the cutouts at the shoulders that were casting shame on the runways and fashion spreads. I had never been a fan of putting holes in my designer clothes.

I turned away from the modern and focused on the old. I didn't know where to begin. I had carte blanche to take whatever I wanted. I felt like Julia Roberts in the hooker movie. Only in my real live version, there were no mean girl retail workers. And I didn't have to sleep with The Arthur to have at it.

I snagged a royal blue cotehardie from one of the racks. I held up the garment to my chest in a mirror. The long sleeves and fitted torso would look good on my body. It was the row of buttons down the front that made me cringe.

Morgan walked over, gave the dress a tug, and

showed me the zipper inside. I squealed with delight and dashed into a dressing room. I pulled off my clothes and stepped into the dress, pleased with the modern enhancements that made the garment easily accessible.

"What do you think?" I said when I stepped out of the dressing room. "Will Gawain be tempted to rip this bodice off me?"

Both Morgan and Gwin had smiled as I stepped out. But they both frowned at my words. I wondered if someone else had their eye on the knight.

"Unless he's already ripping one of your clothes off at night?" I asked.

Morgan wrinkled her nose. "I grew up with him. He's like a brother. The only thing he ever pulled on me was my pigtails."

I looked to Gwin.

"Oh no, no." She shook her head. "I'm married."

"To a homicidal maniac," I said. "No offense."

"None taken." Gwin tugged at her lip as she looked off in the distance.

"I mean, my last boyfriend tried to kill me, too. So, I get it. Well, actually he tried to sacrifice me to a Greek god. But *to-may-toe to-mah-toe*."

Leonidas Baros was the only man I ever claimed as a boyfriend. Likely because he was the first man I ever wanted to be more than friends with. He was my sword master when my dad had been in Greece studying the restorations on the Parthenon. I'd learned most of my moves from Lenny, both vertically and horizontally. I'd fallen hard for that man. Unfortunately, his soul belonged to another man.

No, not in that way. He was a Chosen of the demigod Zeus. Any humans chosen by the Greek gods gave up their soul in exchange for eternal life. Lenny was over a thousand years old. He'd been alive during the Battle of Thermopylae. In fact, he'd led that ill-fated battle of the 300. Did I mention Lenny was King Leonidas of Sparta? Well, that's yet another story.

"But I'm over it," I said. "I'm so ready for a rebound." And I knew just the knight I wanted to bounce around with. Looking at Gwin's shock, I figured she needed to do a bit of bouncing around herself. "Doesn't Merlin's attempt on Arthur's life and his violation of your magic terminate the marriage contract?"

Gwin turned back to me with wide eyes. "Terminate?"

"Yeah. I'm sure that's grounds for a divorce at the least."

I didn't think it possible, but her eyes widened

even more. "Divorce? There's never been a divorce in the history of Camelot."

"But a divorce would free you up to come out of the closet with your feelings for Lance."

"What?" Her hands fluttered like a bird's wing. "No. There's nothing going on between Lancelot and me."

"Do you want there to be?" I hedged.

"When we were children, we..." She looked away. "But we're adults. And I have my duties and responsibilities. I'm still the Lady of the Castle. My people need me. I would never abandon them, not like my husband did."

Her smile was one I'd seen her put on often. It was a plastic smile. The one I'd seen her give to a group of frat boy tourists last week when they had gotten rowdy at the sword in the stone exhibit. She hadn't cracked under them, I knew I'd fare no better. So I turned to Morgan.

"What about you? You have your pick of the knights."

"I would never," she wrinkled her nose. "As soon as they catch Merlin, I'm off to university. I'll find myself a tweed wearing, four-eyed tenured professor and settle down."

"You can't live off a ley line at your age," I said.

Morgan was pushing one hundred fifty in human years. She could spend days, weeks, maybe even a couple months off the line. But if she spent much more time than that off the line, her true age would catch up with her and she'd die.

"Cambridge is on a line. I'll be fine."

I felt a pang in my heart. I hated to see her go. But that's what families did in my experience. They all eventually died or sent you away or left you behind. Boyfriends and friends, too.

I'd never been the type to have a group of girl-friends. I'd never clicked with cliques. Never strutted with a squad. The one time I'd tried had been a life-scarring disaster. It happened at boarding school.

Having traveled all over the world I had a broad fashion sense. I wore a hijab when I was eight because I thought it was a crown. I wore kente cloth as a cape when I was ten. I rocked saris as magical robes at twelve. I often mashed these styles up.

When I went to boarding school as a teen, I brought all my clothing with me. We were allowed to wear what we wanted after school and on the week-ends. In most of the cultures I'd visited, women dressed either modestly or bared their chest. I had yet to wear skirts and shorts or heels or any underwear, but that's what all the popular girls were wearing.

I was more fascinated by Dilawar and her colorful hijabs. We instantly clicked. Then just as instantly, we were targets of the meanest clique.

Erwen Reilly had firebrand red hair and sea green eyes and she was the Queen B of the school. I'd watched armies line up behind generals, I'd watched tribes get in line behind rulers, but I'd never seen the power that Erwen commanded over the girls of the school. She had everyone under her thumb. Except for me and Dilawar.

I didn't step in line behind Erwen because whatever perfume she wore always gave me a headache. But even though I didn't want to stand behind her, it didn't mean I didn't admire the girl's fashion sense. Erwen was always decked out in whatever the models in *Teen Vogue* were wearing. Day by day, I began putting away my traditional garb in favor of what was in the magazine spreads.

Along with Erwen's high-end wardrobe, came a mean streak that didn't often have a rhyme or reason as to who she'd target. When her target became Dilawar and her modest clothing, I stepped up to defend my friend. Unfortunately, I'd been in my first ever pair of heels. As I rushed in to rescue my friend,

I fell promptly on my ass and my Guess ruffled jean skirt flew over my belly.

Did I mention that underwear was a new thing with me as I began my time in boarding school? The binding scraps of cloth made sense when wearing shorts or pants. But I hadn't bought into wearing them under skirts.

When I went to step in and be a hero, it also happened to be one of my commando days. So when I say I fell on my ass, I mean it in the total, literal sense. I was henceforth known as Loren Van Ass.

The teasing was relentless for both Dilawar and me. Dilawar was pulled out of school the next week. Her father, who had not wanted her attending school in the first place, had found a husband for her. She was married at the age of fourteen. I endured a few weeks of that place before working damn hard to get kicked out and sent back to my dad who was on a dig in Rwanda during the country's civil war.

I'd dressed in designer clothes after that for fear of the next mean girl that might come my way. But I still had an eye for the exotic and the vintage. The shop Gwin, Morgan, and I were in would've made a cosplayer wet their bed while wide-awake.

The fine silks made my mouth water, and also

made me wonder if the worms were somewhere in the shop. The lace sandals were seriously working my shoe fetish. I pulled out a flowing headdress that reminded me of my days as a hijab-wearing, super-hero princess.

Morgan headed into a dressing room. Her arms were full of shirts, pants, and gowns as she prepared to do the damage she'd promised Minerva she'd do to Arthur's accounts. Gwin trailed behind her with a single, modest dress. I turned to look at myself in the full-length mirror. I looked the picture-perfect medieval miss with the long sleeves and flowing skirts.

The bell over the shop rang while I continued to admire myself. I knew it couldn't be Minerva back after only twenty minutes. It must be another person from town or a lost tourist. I turned to greet the newcomer with a smile. But my grin fell, my nose twitched, and I felt the beginnings of a migraine.

Through the doorway walked Erwen Reilly. I'd recognize that red hair anywhere. She wore a Versace top over designer jeans. She was no longer in kitten heels, but Louboutin shoes, this year's collection. And apparently, she still wore that same nauseating perfume.

I clutched at my stomach as she came nearer. I

looked down at myself in the medieval garb. Her eyes connected with mine and I felt thirteen again, entirely vulnerable in my bare feet without a New York or European label on my back. At least I was wearing underwear this time.

"Hi," she said smiling brightly.

I blinked. I'd heard that many people changed after high school, some even became decent human beings. Could the impossible have happened? Had Erwen Reilly grown to become human?

"I'm hoping you can help me," she said. "The Visitor's Center is closed for lunch, like we're in some backwater town in the American Bible belt."

Her nose crinkled. She brought her elbows in as though the dust in the place might contaminate her. Nope. Didn't sound like she'd changed a bit.

"I have an appointment with a Ms. Gallahan. She sounded pretty senile on the phone. You wouldn't happen to be her? Would you?"

"No," I managed to bite out.

Erwen looked me over, taking in the peasant skirt, long sleeves, and headdress.

"These aren't my real clothes." I went to pull up the skirt to reveal my jeans. Only to remember they were back in the dressing room.

"Oh my god, we're being flashed," said the

woman beside Erwen. I recognized her as Ruith Doyle, Erwen's longtime partner in mean-girl crime. "I don't want to see elderly cellulite."

"No, no." I dropped my skirt. How was this happening again? These girls came my way and I ended up showing them my ass. Literally. Well, at least they didn't recognize me. I hadn't reminded them of my name.

Gwin stepped out of the dressing room. "Loren? What's going on?"

Crap.

**5**

———

*I*'d always sworn to myself that if ever I came face to face with these girls again I'd be in designer clothes and on the arm of a billionaire. But that wasn't my luck. Instead, I was out in the middle of nowhere Britain, dressed in a medieval gown like some cosplayer, and there were no rich men around.

Why hadn't they come to Greece last month when I'd been on billionaire playboy Tresor Mohandis's yacht? I'd been hanging out in the Royal Olympic Hotel's penthouse with Nia and the Greek gods wearing boutique wares from exclusive shops. I'd been hanging with the world's most powerful superheroes, saving humanity just a couple of weeks ago.

But no, my school nemeses had to do a drive-by when I'd been demoted to an errand girl.

It had been over ten years since last I saw these girls. After falling on my ass one week and losing my friend the next, I had decided I was no longer staying. That was likely when my bad girl persona was born.

I began mouthing off to teachers. By mouthing off I meant demonstrating my superior intellect and wit. Though I was thirteen, I'd been raised by two highly educated individuals and was operating at a college freshman academic level. Plus, I'd been around the world and seen that the so-called facts in the history books were nothing but propaganda and lies. But my history teacher simply sent me to detention in the library with the offensive textbook.

I insisted on playing sounds of the safari in my dorm room at night. I swore with a straight face that the elephants' honking mating call was the only way I could get to sleep. After having my fifth roommate transfer, they left me to bunk by myself in a small room near the attic.

It was in chemistry class that I finally found my out. The idiots had the stupid idea to give adolescents potassium chlorate to scientifically investigate. I knew that if the chemical mixed with certain food products an explosive reaction could occur. Luckily, I'd been sneaking food out of the lunchroom for some time.

A few grams of the chemical, a handful of gummy bears, mixed with a blast of gas from the Bunsen burner, with the oxygen collar up a little too high, and boom. I blew the windows out -after landing on my ass again. I was out on my rear by lunchtime.

My time at the school had been epic. I knew no one would ever forget Loren Van Ass. And now I was facing the music. At least I was standing on my feet to face Erwen and Ruith and not looking up at them from down on my backside.

I couldn't slink away out of the shop. Gwin had just outed me. I knew that at any moment all the memories would flood back into Erwen and Ruith's mind and I'd be a laughing stock again. Well, I'd simply have to face this head on. Hell, I'd faced off against the deranged Titan Cronus and survived. I could handle this.

"Yes," I said with my chest puffed up and my head high. "It's me."

"Oh good," said Erwen. "You're Ms. Gallahan."

"No." My shoulders deflated around the tightening in my chest. They had to remember me. I'd been epic. "I'm Loren. Loren Van..." But I couldn't bring myself to say it.

Erwen turned her head away from me to look over her shoulder. "I told you," she stage-whispered to Ruith. "Senile."

"I'm Ms. Gallahan," said Gwin, stepping up beside me.

Erwen and Ruith turned and appraised Gwin. In unison, their gazes flicked down to the floor and did a quick scan of the woman before them. Gwin was dressed in the same medieval garb as me. But it worked for her lithe, catwalk-ready body.

By the time their gazes reached Gwin's face, there was a slight light in each woman's eyes. Gwin's style choices had been picked apart, but I could tell that the verdict given by Erwen and Ruith wasn't the label of *tragic*. The cool assessment on their faces read to me that they thought they could wear the look better.

What the hell? I was wearing the same style. Just in a different color.

"You must be Ms. Reilly." Gwin stepped forward and reached out her hand. When Erwen came forward and took Gwin's hand, Gwin's shoulders tensed. There was a slight intake of breath. Her gaze went to Erwen's necklace.

It was only a flicker, but I saw a cloud pass over Gwin's face. Erwen saw it too. The corner of her mouth ticked up in what I could only describe as a sinister grin. She reminded me of a predator that watched as its prey saw that it was cornered.

Gwin stepped back. She placed that hand that she'd taken back from Erwen behind her back. She was standing slightly in front of me so I saw her clench and unclench her fist. But standing before the two outsiders, Gwin morphed into hostess mode.

She plastered a fake smile on her face and spoke in the dulcet tones of a travel guide. "You're here for the tour of the Arthurian Legends?"

"No," said Erwen, the sneer still in place as she faced off against Gwin. "We're here to excavate at Caerleon castle."

Behind her back, Gwin fisted her fingers once more. But the serene smile stayed in place for Erwen. "I'm sorry. There must be some misunderstanding. Caerleon castle is deemed historical. There's no digging allowed on the property. In fact, there's no one allowed physically on the property. It's not structurally sound."

"We're not digging. I'm a geophysicist. That means I look for signals underground without turning a rock." Erwen's tone was laced with condescension as she toyed with the vibrant, azurite stone at her neck.

I winced as I watched her. Gwin did too. That's when I recognized what it was— a bluestone.

When I was a kid I'd wanted to go to Stonehenge, but my mother wouldn't allow it. She'd given lame excuses about crowds and bad weather and allergies. After she'd passed away, my father took me there. Before we'd even gotten out of the car, I'd started throwing up. The same thing had happened when we were in South Africa at another stone monument.

Both Stonehenge in Wiltshire, and the stone monument in Johannesburg, and the Drombeg Circle in Ireland weren't just celestial markers minding the longest and shortest days of the year. They were places humans used to ward off witches and sacrifice them. At each of those places were bluestones.

The stones were rare, but they were an anathema to witches, our own personal form of kryptonite. And now I realized that's why I'd always felt off around Erwen. She'd always worn that necklace, meaning she'd always been radioactive.

"My colleague here is an osteoarchaeologist," Erwen was saying.

"It means I study ancient bones," said Ruith, her tone an echo of the lofty airs Erwen put on.

"Study them for what?" asked Morgan, coming up behind us.

Morgan had chosen the Prada skirt and blazer with an alligator pump. She looked every bit the hip, stylish professional. We were the same size. Never had I ever wanted to raid someone's closet as I did now. But this wasn't the time to ask to borrow her blouse.

"In addition to the possible Arthurian connection," said Erwen, "there are rumors that there were witch trials here in the past. We're trying to determine if that was true and if there were any witches buried here."

The polite smile stayed plastered on Gwin's face. Morgan glared, clearly she would lose at any poker game. My expression was blank confusion. I played a convincing ditz from time to time. But this wasn't one of those times. I had no idea what Erwen was on about.

"Ladies," said Gwin, a trickle of laughter in her voice. "You're scientists. Surely you don't believe in the existence of witches? Tell me, did you see the Loch Ness Monster on your way here?"

But Erwen would not be swayed by Gwin's

attempts at humor. Though she and Gwin were the same height, Erwen managed to look down her nose at Gwin.

"All women have a connection to nature," said Erwen. "The moon rules our menstruation. The tide pulls at the chemical composition of our bodies. The seasons change our moods."

Wow, that sounded poetic. My blank expression slipped to admire the thought. But only for a moment.

"There are some women who stole more than their fair share of that connection from Mother Nature," Erwen continued. "What do you think was in that apple that Eve ate? The serpent has been playing us since the beginning."

Okay, now she was veering into Lala Land. Was she serious with that Eve and the devil diatribe? She had on Louboutins and this is what she was doing with her life? What a waste.

"Well," said Gwin, "I can assure you that no witches were buried on these grounds."

That was the truth. The people of Camelot burned their dead so that the magic would disperse back into the ground and rejoin the ley line. Or they transferred it to another person, which was rare.

"Listen, ladies," said Gwin. "Let me change my

clothes, and I'll show you around." Then she turned, corralling us back into the dressing rooms.

We made our way into the back leaving Erwen and Ruith to look around the store with disdain all over their overly-made-up faces. Although that shade of blue on Erwen would so compliment my skin tone.

Morgan's yank on my arm brought me out of my reverie. The three of us crammed into a single dressing room as Morgan faced her sister.

"You invited witch hunters here? Arthur's gonna have a cow."

"On the phone, they said they were scientists researching the legends," said Gwin. "I thought it would be good for tourism."

"Can we back up a second?" I asked. "There are witch hunters?"

"We've always been hunted," said Morgan. "By religious zealots, power-hungry rulers, and now cable television."

"Those women are priestesses," said Gwin.

"Not just any kind of priestess," said Morgan. "They're Banduri."

"What's a Banduri Priestess?" I asked.

"An order of Druid Priestesses," said Morgan. "In ancient times, they were revered for their intellect and their mastery of the sciences and the stars, as well as their alchemical and medicinal knowledge. Their backstory is much like the Amazonians in the *Wonder Woman* comics. The Banduri were fabled to have come from an island near the Loir River. The Celts were so impressed with their beauty and their brains that the Banduri took up leadership roles in the society. Until Rome invaded."

"The Romans eradicated all forms of Druid life in favor of their gods," said Gwin as she finished shimmying out of the store's dress and reached for the gown she'd come in with.

"So why are the Banduri so venomous against witches?"

"It's just like the redhead said, they believe witchcraft started when Eve ate of the Tree of Knowledge," said Morgan. Unlike her sister, Morgan didn't change clothes. In fact, she ripped the price tag off her garment. "The Banduri believe the tree is how we got our powers and that we effectively stole it from nature."

"I haven't heard about one of their kind coming around in hundreds of years," said Gwin as she smoothed her dress down. "We believe that it was the Banduri who built Stonehenge. Ms. Reilly had a bluestone. Did you see it?"

"See it?" said Morgan. "I felt it like a kick to the gut."

"Yeah, she's had it since she was a teenager," I said.

Erwen Reilly, a high priestess? I shouldn't be surprised. She certainly put on airs like she was above everyone else.

"You know that woman?" asked Morgan.

"She was the resident mean girl at my boarding school. She's evil incarnate. Can we turn her into a toad?"

Morgan cocked her head in consideration.

"No," said Gwin. "We can't let on that we have any powers. Or that witches, wizards, and the Arthurian knights are real. You now that."

"Priestesses travel in packs," said Morgan. "We see two but there are more where they came from. They're like women's lib on crack-laced estrogen. I'll go ahead to the castle and warn Arthur."

Morgan stepped out of the dressing room and headed to an exit at the back of the shop. In the Prada skirt and blazer, mind you. I unzipped the cotehardie and stepped out of the dress. It had lost its luster after Erwen's gaze had dismissed it. I stepped back into my jeans and t-shirt.

"We have to appear as normal and as boring and as drab as possible," said Gwin.

I grimaced as I followed her out of the dressing area. Normal? Boring? Drab? Those were all the polar opposites of my personality.

## 6

Caerleon was once a Roman stronghold. From as far back as time was told, Caerleon had been a settlement of farmers. It was filled with grasslands, hills, and patches of scrubs excellent for grazing. Somewhere before 100 A.D., it became a base for a Roman legion. The fortress was built on the end of a low ridge at Lodge Hill and stretched down to the River Usk, which produced a natural defense above the floodplain near the mouth of the river to allow supply to come via the sea.

Most tourists visited the area to see the remnants that the Roman legionnaires had left behind. The sites were basically mossy stones that outlined a bygone era. The barracks looked like a dirty garden with patches of dirty brown, muddy brown, and a hint of sandy brown in some sections. The drill halls provided much of the same view. There was an amphitheater, which I'm sure was something to see when the Romans held gladiatorial shows, but it was just another pile of stones now. Even the temples to Diana, Jupiter Dolicheius, and Kithras were lackluster.

Gwin walked about the town waving her arms as though she showed off the Roman Colosseum. She flicked her wrist, waving her fingers as though she were a game show host showing off the all-expenses paid luxury vacation to the contestants. Erwen rolled her eyes and fixed her gaze on the castle in the distance. She and Ruith clearly had no interest in the ancient Roman sites or sights.

The four of us walked through the town square on the mostly deserted street. A few people milled about during the lunch hour. Most of the town's inhabitants were still at the castle for the communal meal, but a few had begun trickling back to their homes and places of business. The handful of tourists took one look at the closed for lunch signs in the shop and the barren streets and headed back to their rental cars.

"Huh," sniffed Erwen. "It's a charming little town. Quaint enough to want to stop and see. But rustic enough to not want to stay. But, it's cute. Really."

Gwin only smiled, but she also looped her arm through mine, like she was holding me back. I felt instantly chilled. I also felt a tingle, like my cousin had used some sort of calming magic on me. Had she known I was quickly losing my cool and my hands were heating at Erwen's passive-aggressive jab on my newly adopted hood?

"It's true," said Gwin. "Life hasn't changed much here. We are but the descendants of Romans, still sequestered in our little corner of the world as though war rages on outside our fortress."

"Clearly," said Ruith.

There were no Roman descendants in this village. There were no humans either. These were all magical folks.

Gwin smiled passively at me, her eyes sharp, her message clear. I understood that we couldn't let Erwen and Ruith know that. We couldn't let anyone outside our community know that. Witches, when found out, did not fare well through human history. Ever heard of a little town called Salem? Yeah.

"We're mostly farmers now," said Gwin. "Here's our general store. It's filled with locally grown produce."

On display were pointy, green artichokes, fat, purple eggplants, fall-colored gourds, and leafy rings of cabbage.

"You must have some seriously magical soil." Erwen picked up an avocado. "Or these must have cost a fortune to fly in."

The fruit-bearing trees were native to subtropical climates. Which Britain was not. It was hard enough work getting a pit to sprout, growing it into a fruit-bearing tree was a daunting task.

Erwen toyed with the green leaves of the single-seeded berry that would have never survived air travel. Her gaze rose back to Gwin's in a challenge. Gwin's smile faltered as she reached for an explanation.

The truth was that the tree was grown here. With her magic and vast knowledge of plants and chemical compounds, Morgan could make anything placed in soil thrive. There was an avocado tree along with Rainier Cherry and plantain trees and a host of other fruit and vegetables in the magical soil behind the store.

"It was a science project," I said. "The kids were tasked with recreating the conditions to grow exotic plants in a greenhouse. Can you imagine their parents' electricity bill these past months?"

Erwen didn't even spare me a glance. A smirk spread across her face. I wanted to wipe it off with the backside of my hand. Preferably while my hand was on fire.

I wanted to admit that both she and Ruith were amongst witches and wizards, that there were a group of hunky knights just over the hill. That one of those knights looked at me like he wanted to undress me—even though he hadn't in the time I'd been here.

I wanted her to know that it was she who was the outsider here. It was she who was at the bottom of the social poll in this town. It was she who wouldn't fit in. I wanted her to know that this quaint little town could afford to fill a tub with caviar with the wealth the people had accumulated over the centuries.

I wanted her to see the damn label on my designer jeans.

But I didn't say, do, or show off anything. I had to protect these people, my people, my family. Man, having a secret identity sucked balls.

We all turned to the opposite side of the street as a kid zoomed towards us. The young girl was being chased by two others. It wasn't a malicious chase. All the kids were laughing as they carried on. The young girl leading the pack flew above the graveled way on what looked like a hoverboard, while the other two kids chased her on foot.

To the human eye, it looked like she was on a hoverboard. But she wasn't. The young witch was levitating. Gwin had told me that was a difficult skill that was easy for young witches but adults eventually grew out of it.

As the young witch got nearer to us, her arms windmilled. Her feet pumped the air. Her face transformed from joy to fear as she fell out of the air and crashed down onto the hard pavement.

Gwin rushed to her side. The girl had landed on her front and I could hear the cries as I crossed the street to join them. When Gwin turned the girl over there was a gash on her knee.

Gwin balled her fist as she looked down at the girl's wound. I knew my cousin ached to use her healing magic on the girl, but she couldn't. Not with our audience.

"I can make sure nothing is broken," said Ruith coming over. She pulled out a device that looked like an eighties-style cell phone and waved it over the little girl's leg. Then she frowned. "Actually, I can't. There's too much flesh in the way."

Gwin set the little girl on her feet, placing herself

between the girl and Ruith. "It's not so bad. Go inside the store and get a plaster."

The little girl frowned. I wasn't even sure if they sold Band-Aids in the store. All witches had some healing ability. The girl's face screwed in confusion, likely wondering why Lady Gwin didn't heal her boo-boo on the spot. But she did as she was told and headed into the store.

"Shame about her board," said Erwen.

With the magic gone, the illusion was broken and the board was nowhere to be seen. My gaze caught on the bluestone around Erwen's neck. That little rock of poison was the reason the girl had faltered and gotten hurt.

"Look Ms. Galla-*han*," said Erwen. "We're not here for Romans or groceries. We're here to do an exhumation at the castle."

"An exhumation?" said Gwin. True horror washed over her features. "You want to raise a dead body?"

"You can only exhume bodies for criminal investigation, public health, or at the request of the family."

They all turned and looked at me.

I shrugged at the fact that I knew such gruesome details. "My dad was an archaeologist."

"We have a permit for exhumation," said Erwen. "I'm sure you've heard of witch trials. That's a crime. We think trials may have happened in Caerleon's past. The local authorities issued a special license for our investigation."

Erwen handed Gwin the document, then turned on her designer heels, and began walking towards the castle. Gwin stood rooted a moment as she looked at the document. Looking over her shoulder I could tell it was legit. Her blue gaze sharpened as we looked from the document to each other. We turned in unison in a hurry to catch up with the witch hunters.

"You can't go onto the grounds," said Gwin when we caught them up. "It's dangerous."

Plus, there were dozens of live witches inside finishing up their lunchtime meal.

"We're capable women," said Erwen. "We'll manage."

They continued on past the tourist stand with fliers about the Arthurian Legends, past the fake sword in the stone attraction. When they got to the moat, they stopped. That's exactly what the man-made structure was designed to make the enemies do.

The water surrounding the castle was filthy,

swamp-like. In fact, I distinctly saw a greenish-brown bubble rise to the surface and pop. The bridge was lowered, but the wood slats were rotted through enough to see the bubbling brew in many spots. Or so it seemed.

"That's it?" said Ruith. "That's what we came for?"

They looked up at the castle. To the human eye, it was an eyesore with a crumbling face and weathered turrets. Not the pristine palatial estate that someone with magic would see. Nor the crystal clear waters below the metal drawbridge.

Erwen squinted her eyes, tilting her head left and right. She rubbed at the stone as she did so. Then she took a determined step onto the bridge.

When she did, the waters rose up to her heel. A sluice of water wrapped around her entire foot and gave a tug. And then a determined pull. Erwen's body was yanked down into the water up to her knees, as though someone was trying to tug off her shoe. Because someone was trying to tug off her shoe.

It was Viviane, the Lady of the Lake. I should probably mention that Viviane had a bit of a shoe fetish.

Erwen screamed and flailed her arms. Ruith took a decided step back from her friend and covered her garments as the water sprayed up onto the dry land.

I was lackadaisically debating whether I should step forward or not, when strong arms pulled Erwen up and out of the waters. Her shoe did not come with her. She came to stand on the ground. Seaweed socked one of her feet, but still, it worked for her. God, I hated her.

"Did you miss the signs, ma'am?" Arthur stepped back from Erwen once she gained her balance. "There's no access. This entire area is off limits. The structure isn't safe."

Alongside Arthur came Gawain and Geraint, with Morgan, who'd gone ahead to warn them, pulling up the rear.

"I have a permit," Erwen spluttered as she fought a losing battle with the grime soaking into her clothing.

Gwin handed the document to Arthur, who took it and read. "This is a permit to exhume. There are no bodies buried within the city limits."

Erwen's jaw clenched as though she'd known that piece of information.

"I'll have one of my assistants direct you to the burial grounds which are just outside the city." Arthur handed the document back to her.

"And you are?" she asked.

"Joseph Pendergrass."

"Pendergrass?" Erwen chewed at the inside of her lip as she eyed Arthur, the third of his name, the fourth chieftain of the Pendragons. The expression on Erwen's face said she wasn't buying any of the misdirections these people had put in the way of lesser minds.

Arthur bent his large form down to the water. His back was turned to Erwen but I saw him glaring into the waters. A moment later, Erwen's shoe floated to the top with what sounded like a petulant pop. Arthur retrieved Erwen's shoe from the thieving water witch. He rose and handed it to its original owner.

"You saved my shoe," she said. "How chivalrous of you."

"Try to keep it off private property."

"Thank you, Mr. Pendergrass." Erwen's eyes raked over his impressive size. She spared Gawain and Geraint an appraising glance as well. Then she turned to Gwin. "Ms. Gallahan and..." She stared at me.

Suddenly, I felt uncomfortable under her gaze. I felt myself shrinking as she squinted at my face and then ran her gaze down my body. Oh god, was that recognition dawning in her eyes? No, no, no. Not now.

"Loren Van?" she said. And then her eyes widened. "Wait, do I know you?"

My heart was in my throat, but I pushed the words passed anyway. "I just have one of those faces."

"I *do* know you."

My gaze flew up, looking for an exit. Instead of a way out, I saw the accented eyebrows of Geraint. My heart literally stopped.

In front of me, Erwen burst out laughing. She turned to Ruith, pointing at me. "Don't you remember her?"

Ruith frowned at me. "No."

"Back at school. She tried to play hero to some scholarship kid and-"

Ruith's eyes lit up with recognition. "Oh! Yeah. That *is* her."

"Loren Van Ass."

7
———

*I*'d fallen on my ass in front of everyone. But I wasn't in the lunchroom of a preppy boarding school. Nor was I standing before the moat of a dilapidated medieval castle. I was in a tomb, being yanked up by the hair. The man yanking me was tall, broad, and super strong. He was Immortal, like my best friend.

In the dream, I heard Nia shouting my name. Her face was contorted in horror. But not like when I spilled wine on her silk blouse. When that had happened she'd had a controlled anger as she contemplated how to murder me with her bare hands. Now, her face was a helpless anger as she watched me about to be murdered at someone else's hands.

I felt the dagger abrade my skin. The ripping across my chest felt like my heart was breaking. But my mind was on the blood that spilled down Nia's shirt. That wouldn't come out and she was gonna be pissed.

My life didn't flash before my eyes. Instead, I saw my parents smiling at me. I felt their arms reaching for me. With that thought in mind, death didn't seem so bad. Until I hit the floor.

I woke up in a tangle of sheets on the floor on my bedroom in Tintagel castle. I'd been having these nightmares about what happened back in Sarras every couple of nights. But I wasn't lying when I said that death, real or dreamed, didn't scare me. My parents were wherever death led the dying. So it couldn't be all bad. No, what scared me was the ridicule and heartbreak and downright meanness that came from the land of the living.

I thought I'd been scarred when my butt had hit the floor back in school. But I wasn't after any of those girls' respect. Well, not after my crash landing. After being humiliated, I'd just wanted to survive my education. And then to get the hell out of Dodge.

But being humiliated in front of people I cared about? People whose respect I was trying to earn?

People whose pointed eyebrows I wanted to straighten out? Yeah, that ripped open that childhood scab, poured in salt, and set it on fire.

After the devilish duo outed me and my old nickname, I wanted to run away from Camelot. But to where?

There was no way in hell I'd ever go back to my father's family. Not after being rejected when I'd been sat on their doorstep as a child. There was nothing worse than looking into the faces of people who resembled you and having them give you their backs.

I could go back and return to my bestie's side. Before she'd left, Nia told me she was going home for a bit. But I didn't know where that was.

I still had a key to my last boyfriend's place back in Greece. Lenny was on the run from his boss, so I doubted that he'd be there. But I didn't want to get myself involved in anymore Olympian god drama.

I didn't have anywhere to go that was mine. I didn't own any land or rent any living quarters. My life was a series of storage units, hotel rooms, and friends' guest rooms. This bed was warm and comfortable and mine.

Most of the knights and their families stayed

inside Tintagel castle when they took their seats. My room was in the Galahad wing. Igraine had told me that it once belonged to my mother when her family had lived in the castle. But there wasn't anything left of her inside these four walls.

Gwin had taken this room as a girl. After she'd married Merlin, the room had been stripped of her personality and left untouched, likely waiting to be filled with her children. But Gwin and Merlin had had none.

There were no young people living in the castle. The squires went home each night to their parents. Morgan's room was just on the other side of the hall from mine.

Morgan knocked on the door the next morning following my humiliation when I didn't come down for breakfast. Gwin brought food and gave me a hug. Morgan tried to teach me how to do a hex, and when I failed, she also gave me a hug. I'd forgotten how hugs eased pain. Especially when they were from people who weren't trying to get in your pants.

By lunch, my soul was soothed by my cousins, but my ego was not. Theirs wasn't the respect I was after. Finally, I got up and left my room.

I walked down the narrow stairwell, running my hands along the cold stone walls. The stair rungs were the original stone and many of the steps were uneven. But I didn't lose my footing. It was as though my spirit knew these halls.

I knew that the witch whose magic now flowed through my veins had visited this castle when she was alive. The steps, the walls, the tall archways were built by her children. Lady Mary Magdelene was the mother of the true Merlin. Only that wizard was actually a witch. Mara was the wife of Arthur the first. After her mother, she was the greatest witch in recorded history. Many of the acts the storybooks attributed to a white-haired Merlin had been performed by Mara.

I walked through the Great Hall. Up overhead hanging above the archways were flags. Lions, tigers, horses and a few mythological beasts graced the fabrics. These were the flags of many knights who'd been in service to the castle. Many of the lines were no longer. There were only six knights in residence at Camelot.

Walking by the Throne Room, where the Round-table was situated, I found it empty. I slipped across the threshold and came into the room. My grandfather's seat was on the opposite side of the large table. It was bad form to sit in the seat without it being claimed. But there was no one around. I walked over and planted my butt.

The seat felt a little big. It also felt right. Which was scary.

What if I did pass these trials and I took this seat? Did that mean I'd have to stay here forever? I'd never stayed anywhere forever. I didn't truly understand that word; forever.

It hadn't applied to any of my experiences. My life had been one of transience. I'd never had a home. Instead, I'd lived on dig sites with my father. Home was a tarp and a camp chair. I was more comfortable in a tent than on a bed.

That wasn't true. I was more comfortable in a luxury hotel. Or on a yacht. I loved yachts, especially when they were docked in exotic places.

But I'd never stayed in any place for long. I'd been on my own since I was seventeen. And I liked it that way. Less baggage.

Leaning back in the chair, I curled into myself, bringing my knees up to my chin, resting the side of my face on my kneecaps.

Footsteps and deep voices sounded outside the door. I froze in the seat, sinking down like a cockroach on the wall. But there was no way I could hide.

They would see me in here, in this seat that I had not yet earned.

"We think he's in Syria or maybe Turkey." That was Gawain's voice. "He was badly wounded when Gwin cut him with the Spear of Destiny back in Mary Magdalene's tomb. He may have no magic left."

"He may also be dead."

The footsteps came to an abrupt stop for a moment as though they'd all turned and glared at Percy for making that statement. Merlin might be the villain in their current story, but he was still family, their leader's older brother. I'm sure that might be one of the reasons Merlin went AWOL. That and his lifelong illness. Even though he was the elder of the Pendragon brothers, Excalibur, the magical sword, had chosen Arthur to wield it and be the next leader of the knights. Merlin had not only been passed over, he'd been laid up most of his life.

For some reason, a witch's body had no trouble housing large quantities of magic from the ley line, but a wizard's body couldn't handle it. With all the magic that Merlin had been born with, he would've been the greatest wizard of this time. But the power was too much for him. As it began to leave his body, it weakened him, leaching out his life essence as it made its way back to the earth.

Percy may have been right. If Merlin still had an open wound from the god-smashing spear, he had more to worry about than a loss of power. He may have lost his life.

The knights had spent the last few days traveling across the ley lines searching for the wayward wizard. They'd also pulled as many witches and wizards out of remote places as they could for their own safety. The ones who refused to leave they'd left newly knighted squires as guards.

But still, it wasn't enough. No one would be safe until Merlin was brought to justice. Until the Spear of Destiny was taken out of commission.

The Spear of Destiny was the same weapon used to pierce Jesus Christ and hasten his death on the cross. It had been an ordinary blade at the time, but it had been taken by his family and then left on a ley line in the presence of a powerful witch—Mary Magdalene.

Over the millennia the spear had rested, it had gained power from the ley energy, but also from the belief of followers of Jesus and enemies alike that it held power.

It had pierced my Immortal friend's hand and

Nia had bled, which was our first clue to its power. It had struck the heart of another Immortal and left him dead, which is when the alarm bells had gone off in all our heads. That spear, that had hastened the end of the mortal life of Christ, could fell magical and supernatural kind.

Nia had been healed by magic not too long after she'd been cut. Merlin, who'd been pierced in his side by the spear, had not. He'd simply disappeared with the spear while everyone else had been otherwise engaged with saving my life.

"We've checked the Rustem Pasha mosque in Istanbul and the Temple of Bel in Syria," Gawain was saying as they entered the Throne Room. "There was no trace of him."

I knew those holy places were on the ley line grid. Ley lines ran all over the planet and converged at places of spiritual and cultural importance; mainly temples of worship. Faith was a powerful conduit.

"He couldn't have gone much farther if he weren't traveling by ley line and..." Arthur's gaze connected with me and he came to a stop. Like toy soldiers, all the knights behind him came to a company halt and faced me.

I waited for them to say the words that would

kick me out. I could see the words in the twitch at the corners of Geraint's lips. I saw the words in the compassion that softened Gawain's dark gaze.

"Feet off the chair," said Arthur.

I did as I was told. But I didn't get up.

"She should get her *ass* off the chair as well," smirked Geraint.

He looked around, but none of the other knights laughed. Well, Percival eyed me curiously. Tristan turned red. Lance and Gawain looked at Geraint with pinched expressions, like he was the ass.

"If you're going to make fun of me," I said, "at least have the decency to be clever about it."

Percival laughed openly at that bit of sass. Tristan bit his lip and looked down at my boldness. Lance and Gawain's lips twitched at my challenge.

Geraint advanced. Now I got up. But Gawain stepped in front of me. He gave me his back and faced off against his fellow knight. "You're acting like an ass. Don't be a dick too."

"See," I snickered over Gawain's shoulder. "That was clever. You noticed his play on words?"

Geraint clenched his jaw hard enough to hear his molars grind.

"That's enough," said Arthur. He rounded the

table and took his seat. "We have work to do. I'm sure you have squire duties, my lady."

"No," I said, stepping from behind Gawain. "I'm coming with you."

"That's not going to happen."

"You'd all be dead if it weren't for me." I had a scár across my once perfect boobs to attest to it. I wondered if I should yank down my top to remind them.

"No," said Arthur.

"But-"

"That's an order."

"I'm not a soldier."

"Again, that's the point. We are. Your antics might work with Nia, but my knights are a unit."

"You're one for all, I get it." I looked around the room as each man took his seat at the circular table, while I stood on the outside.

"You'll stay here with Gawain and Geraint and guard the castle," said Arthur.

"What?" said Geraint, the smug smile slipping from his face. "Wait."

"Keep up your training," Arthur continued, ignoring Geraint's fuming glare. "Prove yourself."

"Leave Wain with her," said Geraint. "We don't

need two to stay. Camelot has never been penetrated by any enemy."

"Merlin grew up here. He could be targeting the castle." Arthur turned back to me. "You all have your orders. Goodnight, Lady Loren."

I managed not to stick my tongue out at Geraint as I headed out the door. Another victory for me.

**8**

---

*I* leaned against the chair of my grandfather at one end of the Round Table as Gwin stood before an open door at the other end of the Throne Room. The inside of the door was blacker than night. Gwin began a chant that made my blood sing. Stretching her fingers down towards the ground, my cousin called forth the magic of the ley line, opening what amounted to a wormhole, or energy portal, so that she and the knights could pass between space and time and come out the other side at a location connected to the grid.

I'd been through that door before. The trip through a portal was a heady one. It was like being surrounded by every sweet treat you've ever dreamed of, being able to eat them all without any thought of guilt, and then not gaining an ounce of weight as a consequence.

Yup. It was heaven.

But I wasn't going this time. I was being held back and relegated to the bench along with the rest of the second string. Gawain leaned casually against a wall, unconcerned that he was being left to babysit. Geraint, on the other hand, stood fuming. The accents over his eyes were sharp points today while his nostrils flared as he watched his comrades prepare. My fingers curled around my grandfather's chair as I watched Arthur, Lance, Percival, and Tristan line up for the journey.

Percival came to stand beside Arthur, closest to Gwin. Lancelot stood on the opposite side, farthest from Gwin. I saw Lance's jaw tighten when Arthur reached out a hand to Gwin and touched her shoulder.

"Are you sure you're up for this?" Arthur asked.

Now that the ley line was open, Gwin shook out her fingers and clasped her hands together at her middle. Her head turned to address Arthur, but not before her gaze found Lance's.

"We'll understand if you don't want to face him again," Arthur continued.

With the mention of Merlin, Lance looked away from Gwin. She shut her eyes briefly before turning a determined expression to Arthur.

"He's still my responsibility," said Gwin. Then she rushed to clarify. "Not as my husband. I only mean that I showed Merlin this path when I shared my magic with him. It's only right that I be there to bring him to justice."

She snuck another covert glance at Lance. Although her sneaky skills were seriously lacking. Everyone saw it, including Lance.

"You will stay by the doorway," Arthur said, "and stay out of harm's way."

It was only brief, the span of an eye blink, but I saw a look of defiance pass over Gwin's blue gaze at Arthur's order. It was the same look Morgan got whenever Arthur told her to do anything. But Gwin swallowed and the look was gone.

"Yes, my lord." She nodded her head, her voice filled with her normal dulcet tones.

One by one, the knights filed in, keeping Gwin between them. The energy from within the darkness swelled, reaching out into the interior of the room, calling me to step inside. But then the door slammed shut and took all the sweet treats with it.

My shoulders slumped. I was left with Geraint in

the corner. He eyed me with distaste, like an older brother stuck with looking after his annoying baby sister. Oh, he had no idea. I was about to act out today.

"Come along," he growled, turning on his heel and setting a fast pace.

Beside him, Gawain grinned good-naturedly. I got the feeling he saw the mischievous glint in my eyes. Instead of chiding me, he wore an amused look that read *let's see what you got*. He winked at me and followed after his brother-at-arms.

I watched after them for a moment, debating whether or not to follow. But I didn't have anything else to do. I pet the top of the seat that I coveted and then I set off after them.

We headed outside. Once there, we entered into the jousting area. I'd prepared for battle before I'd come down the stairs this morning. I wore a pair of fitted leather pants that doubled to protect my ass as much as it did to accentuate its shape. Over my tunic shirt I wore a light, chain mail shawl that Morgan had fitted me with after I'd risen from the sick bed. The shawl was not only fashionable medieval-chic, it was also magical.

Unlike the medieval knights of history, the Arthurian knights never wore heavy armor. They had no need. It wasn't lances that they faced in battle, it was other magical foes. A piece of steel wouldn't do much to stop magic. It would take magical rings of mesh to ward against the use of a magic object or a wayward witch or wizard that was gunning for you.

The other squires were out in the yard as well. They were all already mounted on horses. Baysle sneered as I walked by, turning to a few of the other squires and snickering. Yuric smiled bright and friendly when he saw me. Maurice nodded his head with a grin. I gave them a wave and a wink. The squires on each side of Baysle perked up at the attention I gave to the other boys and they leaned away from Baysle.

Boys were so easy.

I headed into the stable to mount up. There were no gates on the horses' stables. The stallions were free to roam in and out as they pleased. Their stalls were wide, filled with fresh straw. There wasn't any smell of manure or urine as though the horses preferred to do their business away from where they rested. I'd slept in slums that were nowhere near as nice as these stables.

All the horses stabled were Arabians. Their coats ranged from obsidian black, to a honeyed brown, and a snowy white. A magnificent mare poked her black head out of a stall. Her lips spread as though she were grinning at me. She trotted over to me and bowed her head.

"Greetings, Lady Galahad," she said into my mind. "I am Achila."

It wasn't just the people of Camelot that were magical. Many of the animals were too. It was unavoidable since they all lived on a ley line.

I recognized Achila. I'd ridden her before I'd gotten my powers. She's spoken to me then, but I'd barely heard her voice that first time. Now that my body was filled with magic, I could not only hear her, I could respond.

Well, I could have responded earlier. The horses understood most human languages. But now I had the knowledge that they understood me. Anyway.

"Hello, Achila."

"I have the pleasure of being at your service this morning. I come from the loins of your grandfather's steed, Jasius. Your mother used to ride my mother. I am honored to serve you, my lady."

My mother had been an accomplished rider. She'd put me on a horse when I was six. Riding came to me as naturally as walking. I mounted Achila, feeling immediately at home on her back. We cantered out into the yard and joined the other squires.

"We will continue our joust training," began Geraint. "Remember, the goal is to hit the quintain with the blunt end of your lance and nothing else. Not your head, not your chest. The horses are smart. They will not allow you to hit their heads. They'll toss you first."

I looked at the course. There were two targets. They both were a T-shape on a swivel base. The first had a rig set up with a wooden shield on one end and a tub of water on the other. The second had a similar setup, but in place of the wooden shield was a ring.

Yuric took off first. Holding his lance high, he struck the shield. But just barely. The tub of water splashed down on his back and onto his horse's hide. Snickers rose up from the group of young boys. Yuric hung his head and veered off course, not even attempting the second ring.

Maurice stepped up next. He started his gallop at a slower speed. But his lance didn't quite reach the shield as he neared the target. He veered his horse away from the quintain without even striking it, but he came away dry. Or, so I thought. The tub of water raced after him, splashing down on his head as he came to a halt on the course.

One by one, the boys took their places. They raced for the target and they all came away dripping wet. I was not seeing the point to this exercise. Unless it was simply to entertain those in charge.

Geraint watched the boys intently. His face the same mask of distaste that he always wore. He offered no instruction or encouragement. Not any words at all.

My turn was coming up shortly. I looked down at my leather pants and boots. I hadn't dressed for dunking. Turning away from the course, I caught sight of Gawain. He approached me with one of the wooden lances. There was a smile on his face as he watched me, likely trying to decide what I might do.

"Exactly what is this supposed to teach us about fighting magical villains? I thought we were at war. This looks like play."

"This is tradition," he said, placing the lance in my arm.

"Maybe for the knights of old and the Jedi."

Gawain raised a quizzical eyebrow. I noted that he and Geraint had the same tilt to their eyes. When Geraint raised a brow, it appeared to me as condescending. But when Gawain did it, it was sexy.

"You know," I said. "When Luke has to destroy the Death Star with that one perfect shot? Are we fighting spaceships? Wait, don't tell me there are aliens?"

Before Gawain could answer, Geraint stepped up beside Achila and I. "Has anyone ever told you that you are tiring?"

"All the time." I smiled proudly.

Geraint frowned as though he smelled something foul. Then he reached out and struck Achila's ass. The horse took off.

"Achila," I cried. My hands flailed as she took off at a gallop. "Wait."

"I'm sorry, my lady. He startled me."

"Can you hold on for a second?" I managed to hold onto the lance with one hand and get a grasp on the reins with the other. I pulled the reins but Achila didn't stop.

"I cannot stop now that I've started. We must complete the course. If you don't hit the target you will be splashed."

I tried to lift the lance into position with my one arm. That bugger was heavy. This exercise was definitely sexist as women didn't have the upper body strength of men.

Okay, some did. But I wasn't in that camp. I did

crunches and squats to keep tight and lifted. I gave up on pushups in my teens when my boobs started getting in the way.

Sexist or not, I wasn't going to get the damn lance in place in time. But then I realized, I didn't need manly upper body strength. I had the strength of a witch.

I took a deep breath and concentrated on the lance, trying to imagine the heavy weapon rising into the cradle of my elbow. It didn't budge.

Remembering Morgan chanting over her brew in the kitchen the other day and Gwin chanting to open the ley line doorway earlier, I began mumbling to myself. "Rise up, oh lance." I repeated it three times, really quick. The weapon still pointed limply to the ground.

The target was almost upon me. I was about to get my pants and shoes and my hair wet. But even worse, I'd have to turn around and face Geraint's stuck-up brows.

I huffed out a gush of air in anger. As the air left my body, I felt a surge of energy. Suddenly, the lance felt light as a feather in my arms. Which was a good thing, since the target was right in front of my face.

Achila was going at a full gallop. I locked the lance in place and aimed. The blunt end of the lance hit the target hard enough for it to spin around. I took a second to look up to see that the tub of water stayed in place.

But I wasn't done. I'd advanced to the second part of this trial. The circle was coming up. The hoop was a much smaller target than the quintain. This would take more than magic.

"I am one with the force," I chanted. "And the force is one with me."

I thought of the tiny hole as the disapproving eye of a certain knight. Between the chanting, the visualization, and the remnants of anger, the lance slid through the ring. With the weapon in its mark, I let go of the lance and raised my arms in triumph. I expected groans from the peanut gallery. But behind me, I heard the boys cheer.

I turned to see Gawain clap his hands. Even from this distance, I could see the whites of his teeth flashing in a grin at my triumph. Geraint didn't flash me a bright smile. Instead, I saw the whites of his eyes narrowed into suspicion and disdain.

Achila and I trotted back. The crowd of boys surrounded us. Only Baysle stood apart, looking up at me with the same suspicion and disdain as his lord.

"That was amazing, Lady Lo," said Yuric.

"No one's ever done it on the first try," said Maurice.

"She passed both trials," said one of the squires who'd stood beside Baysle earlier.

"Enough," bellowed Geraint. "All of you. On to martial training."

The boys broke away from me, but not before a few more whispered congratulations. They all fell in line behind Geraint and headed into the armory. I took my time dismounting, unsure if I wanted to face Geraint on the mat or with a weapon.

Achila bowed her head to me before trotting off towards a watering trough. Once again, her horse face was split wide in what looked like a grin. I turned towards the armory only to come face to face with Gawain.

"You used magic, didn't you?"

I shrugged.

"You don't play fair, Lady Lo."

"Not when the deck is stacked against me, no."

Instead of a lecture, he nodded in approval. Gawain was dressed in a loose-fitting pair of jeans today. His tunic shirt was open exposing the top of his breastbone. The divot at the center of his chest reminded me of the markings on the target I'd just hit.

"It could also be because I'm good with holes and sticks," I intoned. I took a step towards him, keeping my eye on the prize, visualizing my hands hitting a new mark.

Gawain's lips parted and his head jerked back. "You have a mouth on you, don't you?"

It was such an easy line to turn dirty. And I wasn't easy. Most days. Instead of responding, I tugged my lower lip into my mouth and then flicked out my tongue.

Clearly, he got the message. But instead of wrapping his arms around me and pulling me into his body, Gawain took a step back. He hung his head and crossed his arms over his chest, covering up the spot I'd been aiming for.

"I can't dally with you, my lady."

"Well, I would hope not," I said. "You look like the type of man that would last longer than a dalliance."

His head snapped up. His lips parted and a gush of air rushed out through his half-hearted chuckle. But he took another step back.

"You're a witch," he said. "Witches deserve forever. I don't have that kinda time to give."

Was he talking about his curse of facing the Green Knight? I still wasn't buying it. I took a step towards him.

But he held up his hands. His expression turned deadly serious. The tone he used when he spoke what little words I let him get out, sounded like the beginning of a breakup speech. A restless ache ran through my right leg. My stomach churned and my head fogged with dizziness.

"Listen, Loren-"

"I was just joking around with you." The words gushed out of my mouth, high-pitched and a touch on the hysterical side. I turned so he didn't see the flush on my cheeks. I coughed and cleared my throat, trying to get back my low and sultry register. When I turned back around, I had my blasé mask firmly in place.

"It's just that I-I'm getting out of a rel-" I choked on the word.

I didn't do relationships. Lenny had been an exception that I had no plans to make again. So what Gawain was rejecting me? At least he wasn't pushing me towards a sacrificial altar. So that was something.

"I was just looking for a little rebound fun," I said. "I can find my kicks elsewhere."

I called to Achila mentally. Thank God it worked. She lifted her head from the trough and trotted back over to me. I hopped back on the horse and took off before Gawain could say anything more.

**9**

—————

*A*chila and I galloped across the land. The stallion asked no questions as she carried me away from the castle. She ran at superhuman, or rather super horse, speed. It felt like we were flying. The wind tossed my hair behind my back. Achila's mane whipped around my face as I let go of the reins and dug my hands into her silky locks.

This felt normal. This felt natural— running. This was my normal response when things went left. I turned right on my heel and ran. I'd been running my whole life, never standing still. It worked for me because I looked good from the back. So, in a sense, my turning tail and running did people a service 'cause they got a look at my perky ass.

The kids at school had gotten a good laugh at my

ass back in my glory days. The science community had seen their fair share when they turned me away every time I tried to clear my father's name. And now, Gawain had watched my seat as I galloped away before he could reject me.

A medical patient could get stuck a hundred times with a needle, but they'd flinch each time the tiny prick broke their skin. No matter what they did, they would never be prepared for that sting. For some reason, I kept offering up my veins. Probably because I liked pricks.

Gawain may have had it right. If I were planning to work with this army of men, I shouldn't try to sleep with any of them. I just didn't know how to be friends with a man.

Except for Nia's ex-boyfriend, Zane. But that was easy since Zane was blind to every woman who wasn't Nia. He took all of my innuendos as jokes. Which they were for the most part. I would never sleep with a friend's boyfriend.

Again.

Don't judge. I didn't grow up in Western civilization. In some cultures, women shared men. I'd learned firsthand that to share a penis was to pave a sharply sloping cliff that led straight to disaster.

I took a deep breath of the afternoon air and

tasted moisture. We must be nearing the river. Achila continued running at top speeds. Being a magical horse, she could last longer than a regular horse, but I needed to stop.

My bum needed a break from all this running. My chest also ached. Likely from the wound of the dagger that had split my heart open a couple of weeks ago.

Surprisingly, dying hadn't been so painful. It had been peaceful. I'd looked up into my bestie's face. Nia had been absolutely panic-stricken. That was cool. I hadn't thought anybody would shed a tear if I'd died.

I'd been surrounded by the knights and Gwin. No one had cried, but they didn't let me walk into the light either. They'd fought to bring me back from the brink of death as I'd almost slipped through their fingers. It had been nice.

Achila slowed as we came to the water's edge. The River Usk bordered Caerleon on the southern border. We were still on the lands of Camelot. A cool breeze blew from the opposite bank, and I shuddered. The air felt wrong from that side. I realized why a second later. It wasn't filled with magic.

I dismounted and went to the water's edge.

Achila wandered upstream a bit to grab a drink. Sitting down on a rock, I pulled off one shoe.

These boots were Alexander McQueen with a studded cap-toe. They'd been in a shipping box yesterday instead of on my feet when they could've done me good in front of Erwen and Ruith. The shoes, along with a good portion of my wardrobe, had arrived from the Netherlands a couple of days ago. But I'd left the boxes be, not thinking I'd need any of my designer wares as I began my training.

With my bum on the cool rock, and the shoe and sock off my foot, I dipped my toes into the water. The waters were cold, but there was a buzzing warmth flowing in the current.

Magic.

I felt the energy soak in between my toes and caress my instep. It felt so good I wanted the full effect with both feet. Before I could reach to take off the second boot, something tickled my bare foot.

I peered down into the water expecting to see a fish. Instead, I saw a pair of opaque eyeballs staring back at me. Long lashes blinked, touching pale white cheekbones. I jerked back, yanking my foot out of the water and coming into a crouch on the rock.

A young woman with white hair emerged from

the water. As her face broke the surface, the droplets of water raced off her skin like tiny beads, leaving her face and hair completely dry. She wore a nightgown, so translucent that if I stared, I could make out the outline of B-cup, pink-tipped breasts.

Her bare feet tread the water as she rested her pale arms on the rocks and grinned at me. "Hello, Magda's daughter."

I took a deep breath as my heart settled. "Hello, Viviane."

"You shouldn't put your bare feet in these waters. There are many magical creatures swimming about. Many who would view human toes as a delicacy, especially witch toes. When you wiggle your toes, it looks like a meal."

Viviane spoke matter of factually. She cocked her head to the side and eyed my bare feet. Her tongue peeked out from between her lips and licked at the corner of her mouth.

"Duly noted," I said, pulling my foot underneath me and scooting farther away from the water's edge.

Viviane was the fabled Lady of the Lake. But she looked like an overgrown kid. Her eyes were bright, like a cat when it flashed you in the night. Her gaze broke from my foot and stared at my one discarded boot with fixed concentration.

"Why are you out here alone?" she asked.

"I wanted some peace and quiet."

"Hmmm. I've noticed the only people who want peace and quiet are the ones who don't have any friends."

"I have friends." I plopped down on my butt.

Viviane nodded, her cat-bright eyes watching as I put my sock and then my boot back on.

"Like the Immortal?"

"Yes," I said, giving my boot a tug until my heel snapped into place. "Nia is my best friend."

"Where is she?"

"I..." I actually had no idea. She hadn't called since she'd left me here to recover. That was a couple of weeks ago now. "She's not here at the moment. But she'll be back... soon."

Viviane nodded again. Her claw-like fingers tapping a rhythm on the rock. "Why aren't you with the knights? They didn't invite you? They never invite me anywhere."

I huffed out a breath. I was beginning to understand why she was short on invites.

"The only time they ever talk to me is when they need a water transport." Her fingers inched closer and closer towards my boot. She extended her index finger and ran it lightly over the leather of my shoe.

"They're off looking for the Spear of Destiny," I said.

"I know." She added a second finger to her foot-fetish exploration. "They're looking in the wrong place."

"How do you know that?"

"Lord Merlin isn't in Mesopotamia."

That word took me a moment to discern. Mesopotamia was an old world term. She meant the Middle East, where Arthur and the knights had gone to look for Merlin. I cocked my head as I looked down at Viviane. She was now fingering the steel toe of my boot.

"Where is he?" I asked. "Where's Merlin?"

"I'll tell you, daughter of Magda." A slow smile spread across her face. "For a price."

Even though my toes were no longer in the water, I felt like I'd been hooked by a sea creature. Too bad for this nymph that I often bit back. "You don't know where the spear is."

Viviane withdrew her hand and it splashed in the water. Her face was the petulant pout of a toddler being denied her favorite toy. "I know exactly where it is. The knights overlooked it, just like they overlooked me, just like they overlook you."

"They haven't overlooked me. They're just

making me jump through hoops like some circus freak."

I looked down at the woman in the water with feet that didn't work and bit my tongue at the remark. She didn't seem to notice. Or she did and didn't care.

"You're going to pass all of their tests, daughter of Magda, because you are the rightful heir to the seat of Galahad. You found the Holy Grail, just as it was prophesied of Galahad, the first of his name. That seat should be yours."

I'd spent a good deal of my life around con artists. Most of them had been my lovers. It's not like I didn't see through their lies. I was just turned on by a silver-tongued devil. Those types of guys had a certain set of skills I appreciated in the bedroom. But I was usually the one stealing out in the middle of the night before he had a chance to work me over outside of the sheets. So I knew when I was being manipulated.

"I can help you take your grandfather's seat," said Viviane. "If you bring them the spear, they can't deny you that seat."

I studied her, but I couldn't work out her angle. "What do you want?"

"Your boots." She didn't miss a beat. She didn't stutter. She didn't sway.

I looked down at my designer boots. They were actually Nia's but I'd snuck them out of her suitcase and into mine at some point. They were her favorites, which meant she had to come back for them.

"If I give you these boots, you'll tell me where the spear is?"

"If you give me the boots, I'll take you to the spear myself. But when we get there you must prick my feet with the blade."

I stood up. My booted foot anchored me to the wet rock. I'd seen that spear make my Immortal friend bleed. I'd watched it end the life of another of her kind. It had incapacitated a powerful wizard. Who knows? Merlin might be dead because of it. Did Viviane have a death wish? As though she read my mind, she answered.

"It is true, the spear killed an Immortal. It also brought on the death of a prophet. That means it's powerful enough to break this curse that was set upon my legs. It will allow me to walk."

"Curse?"

"My father was human," Viviane said simply. "He was afraid of what I was and so he tossed me into the lake. But not before having druid priestesses bind me with their runes."

I gulped. At least I'd been loved by both of my parents. It was just my father's family that had rejected me and sent me to hell, better known as boarding school. And now I was here with my mother's family. They weren't treating me badly, at least not in light of Viviane's past. Maybe I was being too harsh on them?

"Okay," I said. "Why don't I go and get Gawain-"

"No. No knights. It has to be only us."

"Why?"

"You want that seat? When you find the spear it has to be your victory. Men always take the credit."

She had a point there.

"Just you and me," she said. "We'll leave at midnight. Deal?"

**10**
———

rriving back at the castle, I stabled Achila. It was well after lunch as I entered the back door. The dining hall was empty and cleaned. Even though people had their own homes and fully functioning kitchens, everyone still liked to eat together for all meals. It was strange, like an American Thanksgiving three times a day. Except there weren't many arguments. Other than Morgan condescending any and everything Arthur said.

I stomped the muck from my ride off my boots and padded down the hall to the kitchen. I'd managed to not only keep my toes but also my boots after my run-in with the water witch. It was weird that someone who'd never walked or worn any shoes had a shoe fetish. But I guess we all want something outside of our reach. Or in Viviane's case, outside her step.

I didn't know if I was headed back to the waters to meet her at midnight. I didn't know if I would stay here in Camelot through the week. All I knew was that I was hungry.

I ducked into the kitchen expecting to find Morgan brewing another experiment and Gwin watching over her sister's shoulder in disdainful support. Today, Igraine stood behind a stove pinching herbs and tossing them into a pot. The lunch dishes had been cleared and it looked as though she was at work on dinner.

Igraine was the oldest person in town. I'd never asked exactly how old she was, but I knew she was pushing a millennium. She looked like she was in her eighties with her hair faded to a vibrant silver. The wrinkles around her eyes and at the corners of her mouth were wizened. But she was spry, likely from the magic flowing in her veins and living on a ley line all her life. I doubted she'd ever been out of the city.

Her magic was tied to this place. Literally. Along with Gwin and Morgan, she kept up the protective charm over the castle that hid its splendor from human eyes and made it look dilapidated.

Though her magical soul was tied to the lands, I knew that she could leave. Gwin traveled with the knights, opening ley lines and tending to wounded witches. But if Gwin left permanently, it would weaken the charm. Unless another witch stepped up.

"I saved you a plate, dear girl." Igraine pointed a crooked finger at a covered plate on the long, wooden table.

Igraine was also clairvoyant. She could see past events and the future. I knew that some of her visions took a toll on her as they could be a harbinger of bad times. She'd told my friend Nia something bad, but Nia had kept tight-lipped about it.

I sat down at the table and reached for the covering.

"Ahah," said Igraine. "Use your magic."

I blew out a breath, like a child who was told they had to recite their multiplication tables before they could have dessert. I wasn't good at controlling my magic. So far I'd figured out that I could get a burst of energy when I got worked up.

I was exhausted from my ride. But I did as I was told. I concentrated, focusing on lifting the lid from the platter.

Nothing happened.

I tried the trick I'd used in the jousting field and pictured Geraint's face on the metal of the lid. Not a budge or even a rattle.

I pictured Gawain's face as he held up his hands in a stopping motion when I'd made my advances. A chill raced through my fingertips and I clenched my hands into fists. But still, the power didn't transfer to the metal dome.

"You're focusing outward, my dear. The magic is inside you."

What did that even mean? My stomach grumbled in impatience. My temper flared. I shut my eyes.

Behind my eyelids, I saw a flicker. It was the tiniest flame on a cold night. I stretched my hands towards it. The faint heat licked at my fingertips. I stepped closer, intending to grab the flame in the palm of my hands.

Power surged through me. My eyes jerked open. The lid flew up to the ceiling in a loud clang. Then it clattered down on the ground, coming to lie flat now that the dome had become a platter.

I'd never been subtle or measured with anything in my life. It made sense that my magic was loud too. I turned an apologetic face to Igraine.

"You got it off. That was the goal." Her face was

filled with maternal pride and it warmed me from the outside in.

I took a bite of the warm dish. The spices in it reminded me of something my mother used to make when I was a child. I didn't know exactly what it was, but it brought flashes of memories back as I swallowed.

I saw my mother's face smiling at me. I felt her lean over me, the light brush of her lips on my forehead. On my tongue, I tasted the earthy scent that always stayed behind in the room after she'd left.

"Your mother used to sit at that table in that very spot. I think that was her favorite meal."

"I don't understand why she didn't tell me about this place? Or any of her family? Or that she was a witch."

"Magda was a restless spirit just like you. Always looking for greener pastures. She was more interested in history and engineering and art. And she had a science mind, like Morgan."

Behind Igraine, pots stirred themselves without ladles. Sharp knives dashed vegetables on an array of cutting boards. The diced and julienne pieces scooped themselves neatly into mise en place bowls. Igraine, turned to face me as her magic continued to single-handedly prepare the meal that would feed the entire town.

"Magda's magic wasn't very potent, not like her sister's. Gwenfar and Magda had different goals. Gwenfar wanted her daughters to marry the heirs of Camelot, to have high places in magical society. She didn't spend her days dreaming of far-off lands, like her younger sister. Gwenfar spent her days plotting how to capture the attention of the heirs."

And it had worked. Mostly. Gwin had married Merlin. If Auntie Gwenfar had wanted Morgan for Arthur, she must've been disappointed as the two were like oil and water. Ultrafem Morgan swatted away any of Arthur's, or the knights', attempts to suffocate her with their chivalric overprotectiveness.

And now Arthur was preparing to ask for Gwin's hand with his brother turned a crazed fugitive. Gwin would accept. Both of those idiots were so consumed by doing the right thing for their people. Neither thought of themselves.

"I like to believe Magda would've come back when you were a bit older," said Igraine, turning back to check on the progress of one of the pots.

I set my mouth to ask the question I dreaded. "Did she die because of me?"

Igraine stopped what she was doing and turned

to face me. I didn't think it was possible to catch a clairvoyant off guard, but I had.

"Because she left the ley line?" I clarified. "Did her years catch up to her because she wanted to stay with me and my father?"

Humans couldn't live on the ley lines. At least not for long. The potent energy could give them cancer. Most places where the lines converged were sites of holy temples and churches where people visited sporadically or a few times a week at most.

Just as humans couldn't spend a prolonged amount of time on the ley line, a witch couldn't survive more than a few decades off the grid. At least not unless they began siphoning off other witches' powers, like Merlin had begun doing when he'd left.

"Whatever Magda did, it was out of love. She never cast you aside, not like Viviane's parents."

My chest constricted from talking about my mom so I grabbed for a change in topic. "What happened to Viviane? Why is she the way she is?"

"She was born to a human father and a witch. The village brought in priests and priestesses. They burned her mother at the stake when they saw Viviane's deformity. Once they finished with her mother, her father tossed her into the Usk River. She survived because she's a witch, and because those waters are filled with magic. Her body adapted to her environment as she grew."

"She thinks she's cursed."

Igraine sighed. "It's not a curse. It's who she is. You can't change who you are at your core. You can only adapt to what's going on around you."

I saw that penetrating gaze of Igraine's. I knew she often saw things others didn't want her to see. I directed her attention away from myself and onto someone else.

"What does that say about Merlin?"

Igraine smiled sadly. I wasn't sure if it was at my redirect or at the man she once cared for.

"Merlin wasn't born evil, neither was Viviane. Viviane had something done to her by those who were supposed to love her. She decided to make the best of it. Merlin was born ill, but he was loved and cared for. He decided that love wasn't enough. He made a series of choices that led him down a treacherous path."

I'd been lucky enough to have been born into love. The only environment that I'd ever felt that I belonged in was standing between my parents. There was no place like that any longer. Every place I'd been in since their deaths didn't feel right.

Camelot, Tintagel castle, hanging with Gwin and

Morgan, sitting at this table with Igraine all felt good. But not quite right.

"Oh, I know you're leaving us soon, dear girl."

I looked up to Igraine and her penetrating gaze. I opened my mouth to deny it, but nothing came out. I realized at that moment that I'd already made my decision. What she said was the truth.

"But unlike your mother, I know you'll be back. You belong here. You just don't know it yet. Here, dear girl."

She handed me a brown paper bag.

"What's this for?" I asked.

"For your journey. I have a feeling you're going to miss tonight's last meal and I don't want you to get hungry."

I stood to take the bag and Igraine enveloped me in a hug. My fingers dug into the flesh at her back. I held on a second longer after her grip loosened. Then I jerked back at my clinginess. I took the bag of food and headed out of the kitchen.

I was a sucker for taking the easy way out, the path of least resistance, the cheat sheet. I didn't want to do months, years, or decades of squiring when I knew I had the chops to be a knight. I'd already saved the world three times in the last year. So yeah, I was going on a solo tour.

Once I was out of the kitchen, I wasn't sure which way to go? Out of the castle to the waters to meet Viviane? Or down to the armory to check on my duties before heading out. I couldn't bring myself to just cross the drawbridge with unfinished business. I didn't want Yuric and Maurice to have to do more than their fair share of work because I took off without telling them.

"You're still here?"

I looked up and nearly collided with the massive frame of Geraint.

"I thought you'd have gone by now," he said. "You're not the kind to stick around."

"What exactly do you have against me?" I placed the to-go bag behind my back and squared off against him. I didn't want to show my hand that his assumption was right. That would set a dangerous precedence. "Do you secretly want to sleep with me? Go on. Proposition me, see what I say."

"I wouldn't lower myself."

"Well, then you miss the whole point of sex."

Geraint's jaw clenched so hard I heard it creak as he wrenched it open. "You don't belong here. You're not one of us."

"So open the door and kick me out."

"No. You need to leave on your own. Which I'm

sure you will do sooner rather than later. I'll just be there to be sure and check your pockets on the way out."

"You're an asshole."

"You're a thief and an impostor. I looked you up. We do have WIFI here. Loren Van Ah..."

I swallowed, balling my fist in preparation for a swing if he dared call me the hated nickname from my school girl days.

"..Alst, tomb raider, and art forger. Though never convicted. Unlike your father. Something about a dragon bone?"

None of this was as it seemed. But I wasn't about to satisfy this asshat with any explanations.

"I remember Magda from when I was a boy," he continued. "She was a good witch. I cringe to think of how your father duped her. You won't do the same with any of the good people here. I won't allow it. And you'll never become a knight. You don't have the temperament for it. You know it's true."

I didn't have a comeback for his words. Because there were some that I feared might be true. Geraint leaned into me. His cruel beauty made me look away.

"This little talk was just to let you know that I see you. I don't have to do anything to ensure you leave,

I know it will happen. Just don't think you can take anything with you. And that includes Wain."

He had that much wrong. Gawain didn't even want me.

"We'll figure out how to get Lady Mary's magic back from you. You won't be allowed to leave with that either. You'll leave here as you came; a thief with no family and no honor."

I wanted to lash out. But I also didn't want him to know that he'd affected me in any way. It was no matter. He turned on his heel and stormed down the hall.

He had a few things right there. I would never be a proper knight. I was barely a proper lady. And I was going to leave. But not under the circumstances he'd just accused me of.

I was going to get the spear, heal Viviane, and then throw it in all the knights' faces. I didn't need to be knighted to be a hero. Once I was done saving the day, I'd leave this place and go back with Nia, where I was wanted.

## 11

_______

I marched up to my room after the run in with Geraint. Perched in the high-backed chair in the corner of the room was my satchel. It was well worn from ill use, but I always handled it with care. It had been my father's.

Most kids knew their dad was home from work because they saw his car in the driveway. We'd never had a driveway. We'd never had a house that we called our own. We were always on the road or a ship or out in the middle of a desert.

So when I saw that satchel on the tarp of our tent, or in a chair of a rental flat, or on the bed of our hotel room, I knew that my dad was home from work.

He may have been gone for only a few hours, or a few days, or weeks. But seeing that satchel always kicked up my heart rate. I'd race around the campgrounds or from room to room to find him and jump into his arms.

He'd always hold his arms open for me and swing me up and twirl me around, just like in the movies. I'd have his full attention for however long he was back with us. Then he'd always be gone again.

I'm not sure if my mother minded my father's absences or not. She was always as happy as I was to see him. After she died, and it was just my father and me, I didn't let him leave me behind any longer. I latched onto that satchel and would scream if ever he tried to take it away without taking me too.

I placed it over my shoulder now. I'd had the strap repaired twice since the bag had become mine. The zipper stuck. The leather was worn. But still, wherever I went, it came with me.

I stuffed a change of clothes inside. Though I loved my fashions, I was used to living sparsely and out of a bag, traveling on my own, and having my own back. The bag wasn't the only trait I'd inherited from my father.

I'd never been one to fall in for a group hug or make a plan by committee or follow the rules. The more I thought about it, the more I was convinced this Knights of the Round Table thing wasn't for me.

I wasn't going to wait for the other knights to get back to tell them what Viviane had shared. They'd likely try and talk out what to do. Then, in the end, it would likely be that Viviane and I would be left out of the adventure and neither of us would be able to reap the rewards.

I had all the information I needed to give this quest a go. I'd simply go where Viviane took me, get the spear, capture the bad guy, and save the day. Easy.

Then with Merlin captured and the spear out of his hands, there was no reason to stay here in Camelot and face any further rejection.

I wasn't worried about Merlin's magic. He'd already been weakened when Gwin had pierced him with the spear back in Sarras. There had been no reports of missing witches. Arthur had either corralled everyone within the city boundaries or had them protected with squires. So Merlin hadn't replenished his stores of magic.

But still, I stuffed the magically enhanced chain

mail in my bag. Technically, it was mine since it had been given to me. A gift. Not a theft.

With my plan in place, I stuffed my grandfather's sword into my bag. Yuric had fitted it with a cross guard and handle after my magic had melted the cane off. I folded the weapon. It was magical and it bent to my will.

I fussed with the zipper of my dad's bag as it stuck. Usually, I just had to wiggle it until it fell in line. It was being a bit stubborn today, which was fine. In the end, I pulled the teeth as far as they would close and left a small hole open. I pulled the bedroom door quietly shut as I headed out and ran right smack dab into Morgan.

Morgan took one look at my bag. Then her gaze traveled to my guilty expression. Her face transformed from friendly to furious. "You're leaving?"

I shifted the straps of my father's bag on my shoulder and averted my gaze.

Morgan planted her feet in my path and glared at me.

I wasn't used to people checking for me. My first instinct was a flippant remark. But the genuine hurt on her face called me up short.

Morgan was my actual blood family. She and

Gwin were all that was left of the Galahad line. I owed her an explanation.

"I'm not running away," I said. "I'm going on a quest. Viviane says she knows where Merlin and the Spear are. She's going to take me there and I'm going to get it back."

"I get it." Morgan's face softened. She reached out a hand and laid it on my shoulder. "You want to prove yourself to the knights."

"Well..."

"And you're sneaking out because you know they'll try and stop you from doing something so foolhardy as seeking Merlin on your own."

"Um..."

Morgan nodded her head as though I'd answered her in the affirmative. "But you're certain, even though your control over your magic skills are a little less than elementary, that with your combat skills you can take him."

"See..." All of a sudden, I wasn't sure if she was making a case for my actions or laying out the flaws in my plan. I got my answer when I looked again at her blue gaze. Her eyes were dark with fury.

"And you were going to do all of this without me?" she demanded.

Now I winced.

"I'm coming with you." Her eyes were ablaze and her jaw was set.

"Morgan, I can't let you do that."

"Why not? Because I'm a woman? Because I'm a witch?"

Morgan balled her fists at her sides. I felt like a husband whose wife asked if she looked fat in these jeans. There was no safe answer.

"Because..." I began and faltered. "Because you have responsibilities here. You have to hold up the protective shield with your sister."

"Gwin leaves all the time."

"True..."

"I might be anchored to this place, but I'm not handcuffed."

"But..."

Morgan held up her hand, palm thrust forward and her head rolled the entire circumference of her shoulders as she spoke. "If you dare tell me it's too dangerous, or I'm a delicate freakin' witch, or any other chauvinist, chivalric BS, I will reach up and yank out your ovaries."

I grinned. Morgan looked like a fierce Amazonian princess in that moment. All she needed was the headdress and the gold wrist bangles.

"Besides," she said, "that bastard hurt my sister. There's no way I'm being left out of his ass-kicking."

And with that, there was no way I could deny her. Looks like I was about to have a sidekick of my own on my maiden heroine journey. I jerked my head to indicate that she should follow along. Morgan kicked her feet up in a jig, making me wonder if there was any leprechaun blood in our family line. And then I wondered if leprechauns were real?

We headed down the winding stairwell that led to the Great Hall of the castle. I'd learned on my first stay here that this castle was more than a luxurious living space. It was built as a fortress, built to protect the inhabitants. For example, the stairwell we now descended was narrow and uneven so that any assailants coming up the stairs would have their sword arm against the wall and the heroes coming down had their sword arms free. That battle tactic left the villains at an impotent disadvantage.

Coming up the stairs was Geraint, followed by Gawain. Neither knight had a sword in his hand. Geraint held a half-eaten sandwich while Gawain swung the long neck bottle of a beer between his second and third fingers.

Geraint frowned when he saw us. "Exactly where do you think you're going?"

"Just on a stroll before dinner," I said. The problem was that I smiled when I said it. I had the habit of smiling when I lied. Geraint knew I didn't like him. So the moment I flashed my teeth he knew something was up.

Gawain took one look at my satchel. Then he shut his eyes, shaking his head. An amused smile played at his lips when he focused on me.

I wanted to call foul. He couldn't smile at me like that after rejecting me. His intelligent eyes read my face, like they saw the flicker of hurt. His lips parted as though he wanted to explain. I turned away from him in time for Geraint to take a step towards us.

"You two need to get back to your rooms," he said.

"I'm sorry?" Morgan's tone was anything but apologetic. "Exactly who died and made you king of the castle?"

Geraint ignored her and jabbed at me. I stepped back, up one stair rung, to avoid his advance. Unfortunately, I wasn't fast enough. A tomato from his sandwich landed on my shirt, right on the boob. Everyone stared at my chest for a moment.

"Do you know how hard it is to remove tomato stains?" I said.

"No," Geraint said. "But you can report back to me how it goes after laundry duty tomorrow."

I saw red. Not on my shirt. I saw red trickling down to his mouth after I punched him in his aquiline nose.

I didn't actually punch him in the nose. Oh, no. I drew my sword instead.

"Come at me, bruh."

Geraint sneered. "I'm not your brother."

Gawain stepped up until he was on the stair rung beside us. But he was smart enough not to actually step between us. "Calm down both of you. If I'm the voice of reason in this situation, you know there's a problem."

Geraint's eyes narrowed on me. Mine narrowed on him. A dust mote floated in the setting sunlight between us. Instead of a rustle of wind blowing through the standoff, I heard Gawain sigh in defeat.

Geraint reached up to the wall. He grabbed a torch sconce, ripping the metallic shaft off its mount. The torch was still lit as he brought it in front of his body to defend himself. I felt the flame heat the tomato on my shirt, ensuring the stain would never come out.

So that's how he wanted to play it?

Geraint jabbed at me with another of those jerky

thrusts from the first time we battled. Had he learned nothing? How was he a knight and I was a squire?

Then I realized why he fought that way. He was of Moorish ancestry. Those ancient warriors fought with the curved blade of a scimitar, which was a close-range blade. Geraint was used to slashing with his weapon, not thrusting a long sword.

Luckily, he didn't have an actual scimitar. If he'd have had that curved blade it would've done serious damage to the rest of my shirt and everything beneath it. But Geraint was in a medieval castle on a winding stairwell with a weapon that amounted to a sword.

He slashed at me with the iron sconce. I blocked him, throwing him off-center and trapping his sword arm against his body. It's what the stairwell was designed to do in the face of an attack. And he had attacked me. Now he was left open and vulnerable for a kick that would send him tumbling down the stairs.

I looked over Geraint's shoulder. Gawain, who stood in his brother's path, sighed again. Gawain had to know what was coming his way. And he had no time to get out of its path.

I gave Geraint's solar plexus a swift kick with the

heel of my boot. The impact sent him, the sconce, and Gawain tumbling ass over head down the remaining stairs leaving a clear path for me and Morgan.

"Let's go," I called back to Morgan.

She and I leaped over the entangled men and raced through the Great Hall. Behind me, I heard Geraint shouting for someone to raise the drawbridge.

Outside, I saw three figures in the tower that controlled the bridge. Yuric and Maurice hesitated as they heard Geraint's call but looked down and saw two ladies racing for the bridge.

Baysle stepped in. He smirked with glee when he saw me and took command. The bridge slowly ticked up, cutting off our access across the way.

"See, this is when it would be helpful if witches could fly," I said.

"We don't need to fly," said Morgan. "Just jump."

"Jump?" I looked down into the waters of the mote. "Into the dirty water?"

But then a light brightened in the depths of the water. Inside the illuminated waters, which also illuminated all manner of things I didn't want to touch me, I saw a giant bubble. Who needed a bridge when you had a water witch?

We jumped just as the bridge closed. Only the tips of my boots got wet as I landed with Morgan in the bubble. Just outside the bubble, I saw Viviane floating in her white nightgown. Her smile was huge as she eyed my boots.

"Viviane, go!"

She blinked, focusing on me. Then she disappeared beneath the bubble, tugging it behind her, and we took off into darkness.

**12**

———

raveling by ley line felt like falling. But not a free fall like bungee jumping or hopping out of an airplane. I would know. I'd done both.

So let me amend my simile. It was more like riding a roller coaster. When the rider's body gets flung here and there out of their control. But they were strapped in and there was little chance that they'd be thrown free and die.

And it was a thrill. Instead of thin air, my lungs were drowned in the energy of the ley line. It was like a battery recharge and I was already operating at one hundred percent after receiving all of Mary Magdalene's magic. So I felt like I was about to burst with energy by the time we pulled into the arrival station.

It felt like I was falling forward. Actually rolling forward. I hit the ground hard. Water splashed on my face. But amazingly, my shoes stayed dry.

"That was a really rough landing, Vivi," I groaned.

"I didn't get them wet, did I?" Viviane pushed her torso up on the ground, her lower body still submerged in the waters. She bent over inspecting my shoes. Opening her mouth and taking in a lungful of air, she blew. Every droplet of water left my boots leaving them pristine and dry. Viviane smiled at her handiwork.

"We're in Glastonbury?" said Morgan, coming to stand beside me.

I yanked my boots away from Viviane's perusal and looked around. The sun had set. There wasn't much to see in the evening light. In the distance, I did see the remnants of a castle. That had to be Cadbury Castle where my mother had been born. It was formerly known as Camelot.

Ironic, huh? Not so much.

Once upon a time, the Arthurian castle of Tintagel had occupied the lands upon which the current castle in Glastonbury sits. At that time, this whole land had been called Glistening Town. The local people had believed witches and fairies and magical creatures walked the pastures and swam in the waters.

They hadn't known how right they were. Looking at the site now, it was mostly a flat plateau with a few ramparts forming a broken, defensive boundary. But that's what you saw if you were looking at it with human eyes.

In addition to the remnant ramparts, there was also a remnant charm on this place. With the witch blood running through my veins, I saw the shadow of turrets in the horizon. There was the ghost of a drawbridge lowered over the dry land. The revenant of the battlements surrounding the top of the castle faded in and out as I blinked.

But the sight wouldn't stay in focus. The magic was old and there were no longer any witches or wizards in this land to reinforce it. Tintagel and its magic had moved on, leaving this place behind.

There was nowhere for an ailing wizard to hide in this wide open space. There were no resources he could rally himself with. No magical beings he could siphon energy off. So why did Viviane think Merlin was here?

"Arthur said they checked the castle and Merlin wasn't here," I said.

"He's not at Cadbury Castle," said Viviane.

Both Morgan and I turned on Viviane. Did she think this was a game? Because Morgan and I were in serious trouble when we got back to Camelot. Well, Morgan was. I wasn't sticking around to receive my punishment.

"He's up there." Viviane pointed to the top of a hill.

"Merlin's up on the Tor?" Morgan's voice was filled with wariness. Her adventurous spirit suddenly dampened.

"What's wrong?" I asked. "What's up there?"

"Oh, just the stuff of myths, legends, and nightmares."

I looked up at the hill. I knew it by legend. My mother used to read me stories about it.

In reality, the Glastonbury Tor was a lumpy looking land mass with a patched stairway leading to the top. At the summit sat a solitary structure; the Tor. The structure was all that was left of the 14th-century Christian church built for Saint Michael. Originally, the church had been made of wood, but an earthquake sometime in the 13th century brought the holy place down. The church was rebuilt with stone in the 14th century, but it was demolished by human hands a century later. All that remained was the tower, or Tor.

My mother had spoken of this mystical place in some of the bedtime stories she read to me at night. Another name for this place was the Isle of Avalon. In many stories, Avalon was said to be the Celtic underworld where fairies and elves and other magical creatures lived.

"Well if he's up there, then that's where we need to go," I said.

"Please be careful not to scuff the boots," called Viviane from her place in the water.

Morgan walked towards the mist covered hill. This land was once an island, but was now a penin-sula with lakes covering three of its sides. The hill sat on a damp bit of low-lying land. With so much opportunity for condensation, a visual illusion known as Fata Morgana emerged where the hill appeared to rise out of the mists. As we headed towards the base of the hill, the mists began to rise into the night's air now that the sun had set.

"If Merlin really is up there," I said, "he'll see us coming."

"Here," said Morgan. "Let me show you how to shield."

We stopped at a well-situated spring at the foot of the mountain. The Chalice Spring, a placard said it was called. The waters came from beneath the Tor from a spring deep in the ground.

"Magic runs through our veins, much like this well," said Morgan. "And like this well, there is a spring that resides in us where our magic is stored. It's here."

Morgan placed her flat palm on my belly. I inhaled and felt a fullness there at her touch. But when I exhaled, the feeling didn't remain.

"It's in your gut. Can you feel it?"

I felt something in my belly. But I doubted it was a wellspring of magic. My stomach grumbled, echoing in the silent night.

Morgan looked down at my belly, jerking her hand away. Then recognition dawned in her dark blue eyes and she rolled them, making a clucking sound with her tongue.

"What?" I shrugged. "I missed dinner."

"Fine, I'll shield us both. Come here."

I came to stand next to her. She closed her eyes and took a deep breath. I felt something push at my shoulder and thigh, but when I looked down I couldn't see anything solid.

I blinked my eyes a couple of times. Finally, the

veil fell off Morgan's magic and I saw a golden mist swirling from her belly and reaching out to surround the both of us. It was much like the golden mist I saw around Tintagel when I looked out the corner of my eye.

Once the magic was securely in place and we were hidden from view, we started up the hill. Our steps were quiet but there was still a rumbling sound that trailed us. I reached into my satchel and pulled out the brown paper bag Igraine had seen I'd need.

"Hungry?" I asked Morgan.

She leaned away from me with a pinched frown. "How can you eat that garbage?"

"Oh, I love it," I said taking a healthy gulp of the stew. "My mom used to make it for me all the time."

Garbage, the dish's actual title, was a mixture of all the discarded parts of a chicken; the heads, feet, livers, and gizzards. Those pieces were thrown in a pot with beef broth and a bunch of spices.

The pepper and saffron hit the back of my throat and I coughed. Between my grumbling belly, the slurping of my dinner, and the subsequent choking on my meal, I wasn't making our approach very stealthy. But I knew that the shield applied to sound as well as sight, so I slurped away. I got in a good belch after I was done.

Morgan, who although disdained most acts of chivalry, had at least been raised with manners. Unlike me who'd been a feral thing on dig sites and camping grounds. She shook her head at me, but didn't chide me. Instead, she told me more about the Tor as we climbed to the summit.

"There are tunnels beneath the hill. Legends tell of people disappearing in the caves down there. They say it's the entry into the city of Avalon, the world of the fairies."

"Wait! There really are fairies?"

"They even say a UFO has landed at the tower."

"Is any of that true?"

Morgan shrugged. "I'm sure the UFO bit is likely rumors spread by the tourism board to keep people coming to visit the site. But science junkies and paranormal enthusiasts are their real target. They investigate and write papers and books and television shows. Those are the people with money to spend, unlike the hippies who come to feel the energy of this sacred land. They're usually dirt poor."

I didn't see any scientific or technical equipment or tents out today. Probably because it had rained all weekend and the ground was damp.

"I do know that there are tunnels down below," said Morgan. "But I doubt there's any access to

Avalon. Those doors have been shut for centuries. We believe that's where our kind came from. But they want nothing to do with us any longer. They think witches and wizards are beneath them since we mixed with humans. Plus, they had a spat with Arthur, the first. Legend has it that he was supposed to marry a fairy princess. Instead, he fell in love with Mara. The fairy king never forgave the slight."

My head was spinning as I climbed. Fairies were real? And there was yet another Arthurian soap opera the history books missed. Man, Hollywood would have a field day with these love triangles and tragedies.

"It seems like a lot of that goes on here," I said. "Unrequited love. You don't have your eye on one of the knights? Or a squire perhaps?"

Morgan wrinkled her nose and shook her head.

"Maybe you're pining for another witch?"

"I'm not that liberated," she said, her brows up to her hairline. "And no, I'm not interested in any of the men of our kind. None of the knights or squires will touch a witch without having matrimonial intentions."

"You don't want to get married?"

Morgan shrugged again. "Maybe? Someday. But I'd like to live my life first. I've been on this earth for one hundred and forty-eight years and I've never been on a date."

"Never?"

She shook her head.

"So that means you've never...?"

"Had sex? Nope. Like I said, none of the men at Camelot will touch a witch without first putting a ring on her finger. My mother still has her sights set on me marrying Arthur. I would do anything just to get out from under his tyrannical rule."

"Arthur's not so bad." Not if you liked bulky, bossy, alpha males. Which admittedly was my weakness.

"Oh, yeah?" snorted Morgan. "I'll trade you Geraint for Arthur any day."

I shuddered just hearing his name. Geraint was bulky and bossy, but he had this air of superiority that killed my lady-erection. "It's not right. A man that pretty shouldn't be that mean."

"I've never seen him behave around someone the way he behaves towards you. He's normally very quiet and thoughtful. I know he had a tough time growing up in the 19th century, being a Moor. The world outside isn't as inclusive as Camelot."

Oh, no. She was not about to make me feel guilty for my total dislike of that man.

"But you get under his skin," Morgan continued.

"Yeah, I have a way with men."

I rubbed at my head. Now that my belly was full I felt like I was getting a bit tired walking up the hill. Which was odd. It wasn't that far of a hike or that steep of a climb, but my body felt weary as we neared the summit.

"Man, flying powers would come in really handy right now."

"Flying is possible," said Morgan. "It's just tiring. You're levitating your own body weight for extended periods of time. Someone once built magic shoes that let them fly but the wind resistance messed them up and they crashed. I can't remember if they survived or not?"

Flying shoes might be worth it now. My legs felt heavy as I tried to take the last few steps up the hill. I noticed Morgan had slowed too. She also rubbed at her head.

Morgan and I both stopped mid-stride. We stared at each other. The truth of our predicament came slowly to our foggy brains.

In unison, we both turned our gazes to the top of the hill. We took the last few steps to bring us to the summit. Those steps felt like we were slogging through chest deep water. It wasn't blue water that weighed us down. It was another blue substance. At the top of the hill, I came face to face with my worst nightmare.

"We know you're there, witches," said Erwen. "Double, double, toil and trouble. Come on out of your magical bubble."

## 13

A group of twenty women filed out of the Tor. Their catwalk was pagan chic as long, tall wispy woman after lithe, statuesque svelte woman glided towards us. They were dressed in flowing robes that showcased their toned thighs. Their feet were sandaled in stylish silver and gold slippers. On their heads were crowns of leaves.

But they gave away their true century with their accessories, including a Rolex watch on one woman and a fitness tracker on another. One had a blue tooth in her ear. Around each of their necks, they wore a bluestone locket.

"Oh, hey," said a brunette with irises that matched the stone at her chest. "I remember you."

I remembered her too. Thalia used to strut down

the hallways with Erwen and Ruith back at boarding school. I cringed, waiting for her to call out that cursed nickname.

"Loren, right?" Thalia aimed a genuine smile at me.

Thalia had always been nice where Erwen and Ruith seemed to like to watch others writhe in pain. But I'd always assumed Thalia's niceties were due to her, let's call it, airiness.

"It's so good to see you again, Loren. It's been forever."

Thalia opened her arms and took a step towards me. I stepped back as that cursed stone came in closer proximity to my skin. My gaze was fixed on it, not her. Thalia stopped, looking from her chest to mine.

"Oh, no, Loren. Don't tell me you're a witch?" She covered the stone on her chest with her hand. Her face contorted from welcome to somber, as though she'd just discovered I had a terminal illness. "I'm so sorry for you. And you were such a nice girl."

Yeah, she didn't know me very well. No one who knew me back then, or now, for that matter, would put my name and nice in the same sentence. But Thalia had always seen the world through a kaleidoscope perspective. Seeing it in colorful, fractal pieces.

As much as Gwin and Arthur had tried to conceal what we truly were when Erwen and Ruith came to town, I didn't think I could deny my true identity any longer. The effect their blue kryptonite had on me was visible. And there was the matter of appearing from thin air once Erwen had metaphorically popped Morgan's bubble.

"Don't worry, love," said Thalia. "We have a way to fix your little witch problem and make you all better."

"Better?" I asked, turning to Morgan.

I felt the tension running off Morgan. It soaked the humid air making the atmosphere dense and taut. Looking over, I also noted that the women had formed a circle around us. Looking out the corner of my eye, I no longer saw the golden mist of Morgan's cloaking spell. We were well and truly revealed. I also felt a heaviness in the pit of my stomach where Morgan had said the well of my magic lay. It was as though I was lugging around a fifty-pound dumbbell.

"The Banduri believe witches stole their power," said Morgan through gritted teeth. "They've been searching for ways to give that power back to the earth."

"Ways like how?" I asked.

It was rude, I know, to talk about these women as though they weren't there. But none of them jumped in to answer. They each eyed Morgan and me like we were a science experiment they wanted to dig their manicured nails into.

"Ways like burning witches on a cross," said Morgan.

"Oh, no, dear," said Thalia. "We believe all life is precious. We don't practice sacrifice. Not anymore. We voted. Our new motto is cure, not kill. Right, Erwen?"

I looked to the center of the group. I expected Erwen to be eyeing me now that I'd pulled a witch card out of my hat. I'd wanted to reveal myself back in Camelot but wasn't able to. Now she'd see me as I truly was; a powerful, magical being that she'd have to take seriously. But she paid me no mind. Erwen's gaze was on Morgan.

"What is one from Arthur's harem doing so far from his bed?"

Yeah, that thick air around us in the midst of this standoff? Well, Morgan sucked it all down in a long, loud gasp of pure indignation. Then she rolled her neck and raised her finger like it was an uncocked gun.

"First of all, I am Arthur's *nothing*. I have never been anywhere near his bed."

"Awww," Erwen cooed, pouting out her lower lip in unsympathetic mockery. "You didn't get chosen, sweetie?"

Morgan dropped her finger. Her feet set into motion ready to pounce on the woman. I got my arms around her in time to hold her back. But damn, cuz was strong. She lifted me off my feet as she lunged for Erwen. If my forearms hadn't been wrapped around hers, Erwen might've had that mocking lower lip split in two.

"Watch it there, Van Ass," said Ruith. "No one here wants to see your brains again."

I'd managed to step in front of Morgan. But now I wondered if she'd have to hold me back next. "You were always such a bitch, Ruith."

"Um," Thalia raised her hand. "I'm really not comfortable with the B-word."

"I hear you've become quite the slut," said Ruith. "Gotten really good at showing that flat ass to all the knights around, and on, that little table of theirs."

I heaved out a gush of air at her foul, offensive accusation. My ass was anything but flat. Before I could voice any dissent to correct Ruith on the perfectly round proportions of my backside, Thalia stepped back up on the soapbox.

"I'm really not comfortable with the S-word either. Ladies, there's so much aggression amongst young women in today's world. We've become masters of passive aggression, indirect putdowns, and snide remarks."

"Of course there's aggression," said Ruith. "It's how we compete as women. We are intellectual where men are physical. For example, if I break your leg, Van Ass, your cells can heal. If I break your spirit, you're fucked."

Seriously, what was it with this chick and breaking bones?

"Look," I said. "We don't want any trouble."

"Speak for yourself," muttered Morgan. Her dark blue gaze was still trained on Erwen.

"Witches are trouble," said Erwen. "You lot are the first incarnation of trouble back to the time of the Garden when you stole from the very Mother who created you, when Eve took from the Tree of Knowledge."

My mouth went slack at her pronouncement. I remembered Erwen being a top student back at school, excelling in the sciences. Back at Camelot, she'd said she was a geophysicist. I wasn't exactly sure what that entailed, but it had the word physicist in it. That had to mean she was smart? But she bought into a mashed up myth of the Biblical first woman eating a magical fruit?

"I saw evidence of your wickedness in your little town," Erwen continued. "You force vegetables to grow in places that are foreign. You indoctrinate the children to defy the laws of nature. And worse, you allow women to be at the beck and call of a group of men. At the very least, you should be ruling the men."

I chanced a look at Morgan. I'd felt her heating beside me as Erwen went off about her vegetables and the children. But there was a marked cooling when Erwen mentioned the gender roles and leadership. It was only a second, but I was certain I saw Morgan raise a contemplative eyebrow at that last suggestion.

"Okay, let's be reasonable," I said. "It's clear you disagree with our lifestyle choices. Even though you're the ones wearing a polyester blend on the top of a windy British hill at night."

A few of the women took a second to look down at their wardrobe choice. Another shuddered, probably wishing she'd worn a shawl or some fur. The scene reminded me of the line of girls scantily-clad, waiting outside the velvet ropes of a club in the dead of winter.

"But I don't see how you're going to get our power from us?" I continued. "I'm thankful that burning and sacrifice are off the table. So, what? Are you going to dazzle us with your stones all night?"

Erwen smiled and I had to hold still instead of itching at the prickle that began up my spine.

"No, sweetie. We're gonna make this a family affair."

"Family?"

"She's talking about Linny-Boy," said Ruith.

"I thought we decided to call him Merly," said Thalia.

"Merlin? He's here?" I asked. "You have to tell us where he is. He's very dangerous."

"He's as harmless as a fly," said Thalia.

As if on cue, Merlin emerged from the inner structure of the Tor. Merlin was Arthur's older brother by a couple of decades in human time. That would translate to just a few years in ley time, making him appear as though he might be in his early thirties.

I'd seen family portraits of Merlin back in Tintagel. He'd been a thin boy and a gaunt young man as the magic had wreaked havoc on his body his entire life. He looked healthy in his wedding portrait alongside Gwin. Nothing about him had screamed magical wizard, more like math wizard without the glasses or pocket protector. But his face had been fresh with a small glint of vibrancy in his gray eyes.

The man who emerged from the crumbling tower didn't look a day under eighty. Being off the ley line for this extended period of time, coupled with the wound inflicted upon him by his wife, had clearly taken its toll.

Merlin walked with a limp, favoring his left side. I know Gwin had pierced him on the right with the Spear of Destiny. In his right hand, he held the Spear, using it as a cane. He leaned heavily on it as he made his way into the circle.

Had the wound still not healed? When it had nicked Nia's fingertip, she'd bled until Gwin healed her. When it pierced the heart of another Immortal, Yod, Merlin's partner in crime, had never recovered.

"He's not going to hurt you," Thalia soothed. "Merly here has found a way to take that cursed magic from you and give it back to the earth, like he did with his magic."

Give it back? Not likely. Merlin had grabby hands

when it came to other witches' magic. That's how he got wounded in the first place. He'd come to Sarras where Mary Magadelene's body rested. He'd planned to steal the dead witch's power for himself. Now, all that power was coursing through my veins. And I was about to be presented to him, like a Loren-sized crack vile he could hit. But when my gaze flicked to the weakened wizard, he was paying me no mind. He was focused on Morgan.

Seriously? Did no one realize the awesome power that was raging inside of me? Kinda didn't matter while I stood paralyzed in the middle of this power circle.

"We will bring peace," Thalia was saying to Morgan. "We will take the rule from the knights and we will free all of you witches to feel the power of the earth and not the ley lines. You'll thank us."

I didn't know what the heck was up with all the communist magical folks. Arthur and his knights wanted all witches under their watch. And now these priestesses believed magic should be taken from individuals and redistributed back into the earth so that everyone was equal.

Didn't matter. This cold war was about to end. Once I figured out how to denuke the situation.

## 14

"Go on, Merly," said Erwen. "We need to try before we buy."

Erwen grabbed Morgan's wrists. I saw a golden mist ignite out of the tips of Morgan's fingers. But with the bluestone in such close proximity, her magic shorted out.

Morgan turned her ire to Merlin. "You weak, bloody bastard. You know I inwardly cheered when they said you were dead."

"I've never cared for you either, my dear sister-in-law. You know your mother originally wanted Gwin for Arthur and you for me?"

"I would've smothered you in your sickbed long ago," spat Morgan.

"I have no doubt. Hold her still please."

Ruith came up to help Erwen hold Morgan still. Each priestess took one of Morgan's forearms. With Morgan between them as a sacrifice, they turned and peered at Merlin.

But Merlin didn't advance on Morgan. His eyes crinkled like a predator sensing the faint presence of easy prey. He inhaled, like a dog sniffing a particularly juicy bone. Then his gaze turned to me.

He narrowed his gray eyes on me. For a second, I held stock still. His eyes were so like his younger brother's that I felt that same bout of anxiety as when Arthur peered down at me. It felt exactly the same, like Merlin was weighing my worth.

"They gave you Lady Mary Magdalene's magic?"

His voice was filled with incredulity. I suppose that, like his brother, he'd found me wanting.

"Who are you?" Merlin demanded, turning entirely away from Morgan and focusing his whole being on me.

"I'm Loren Van..." I looked around at my youthful tormentors. Then I put my shoulders back and tilted my chin high in the moon's spotlight. "I'm Loren Van Alst; Receptor of Lady Mary's magic, Knight of Camelot, and last in the line of Sir Galahad."

The wind rustled the robes of the women standing about. I heard a few blades of grass rustle with the movement of night crawlers. But other than nature, silence greeted my honorific.

"Listen, Merlin, you don't have to do this," I said. I wracked my brain trying to remember Igraine's prophetic words and repeat them. "You were born ill, not evil. You can choose a different path, be the great, wise hero. Just like in the stories."

Merlin opened his mouth and laughed. It wasn't the evil, cackling laugh of a villain. It was the wet, congested hacking of an old, dying man. His gray eyes looked through me, like they were looking into me. Like they were seeing all that untapped power coursing through my veins.

"Forget that one. Let's start with her." Merlin pointed a crooked finger at me with one hand, while he gripped the spear with the other.

"You're making the biggest mistake of your life, Merlin. If you turn your back on your family there's no turning around." I know that directional statement didn't make sense, but my brain wasn't operating at peak performance in this moment of duress. I tried to take a step back, and then I felt a dagger at my back.

"Don't be brave, Van Ass," said Ruith.

Erwen still held onto Morgan. And by held, I mean Erwen pressed Morgan's back to her chest.

Ruith tossed Erwen her necklace, which Erwen promptly held up in Morgan's face. Morgan's expression was contorted in agony with the bluestones so close to her person.

Ruith was stoneless, but she had steel on me. She walked me out of the circle with Merlin. Even though the stones were still many and near me, I felt like I could breathe again. Until Merlin began to chant.

I remembered Merlin's chant when he'd tried to take Gwin's power back in Sarras. When he'd done that, Gwin had levitated the Spear of Destiny into her hand and sliced his side, causing him to let her go. I was still crap at levitation. I could barely manage to get the lid off a dinner plate.

I was so screwed.

I'd just gotten my superpowers and now I was gonna lose them before I even knew how to use them. My dreams of being a heroine were being dashed and I hadn't even had a chance to put together a cool outfit.

I noticed that Merlin was nearing the end of the chant. But nothing was happening. He said the last few words and then he frowned, looking down at his hands. The frown wasn't one of surprise. It was one of annoyed disappointment.

"Did it happen?" asked Ruith, still holding the dagger to my back. "Is he finished?"

"I didn't feel anything," said Thalia.

"Maybe he's impotent?" said Erwen.

"You can't say that to a man, Erwen," said Thalia. "Now, he definitely won't be able to get his spell up."

But Erwen was right. Merlin was impotent. Standing near him outside of the stone circle, I didn't feel a slight hum of magic coming from him. So, the spear had taken it all. If he had no magic left, his spell to steal mine wouldn't work.

Ha! Karma was a bitch.

Merlin looked at the spear as though to confirm my thoughts. Before he lowered his hands, I noted a trail of blood at his side. It appeared through the fabric of his long tunic shirt. His wound from the spear hadn't healed.

I felt the knife at my back slack as Ruith took more interest in him than in me. I was outside of the circle. Everyone's attention was momentarily diverted. I might not be able to use my magic well, but I knew how to use my fists.

It was now or never. Time to do something heroic. I just hoped it wouldn't get me and Morgan killed in the process.

I whirled around, trapping Ruith's forearm in the

crook of my elbow. It was a martial arts move I'd seen watching Kung Fu movies. No one was more surprised than me that it worked.

Ruith's eyes were wide with shock. I stripped the dagger from her hand and then thrust my elbow back, clocking her in the face.

Unlike Thalia, I did condone violence. I'd taken to sword fighting as a child. I'd been brawling and fighting my way out of hairy situations since I'd been on my own. But that punch I'd just thrown, the one that bloodied Ruith Doyle's nose job, I would never forget that for the rest of my long life.

'Cause my life would be long. I had the upper hand now and Ruith's dagger. I twirled it in my palm, feeling like I was the queen of the hill. Until I saw the spear aimed at Morgan's gut.

"I know my Biblical history," said Erwen. "I know Mary Magdalene was a witch. I know the man she married, Joseph of Arimathea, the uncle of Jesus Christ, was also the man who took his body from the cross. Along with the spear used to end his life. You were holding out on us, Merly boy."

Merlin's hunched body stood by the scene. His gray eyes were glassy and his hands were empty. Erwen had the spear. The sharp point of it had already torn a hole in the bodice of Morgan's shirt.

"This is the Spear of Destiny."

Merlin's jaw clenched. Even with his aged face and long scraggly hair, the expression on his face reminded me of Arthur when he argued with Morgan and she made an irrefutable point.

"A god killer," continued Erwen. "A witch slayer."

Out of the corner of my eye, I saw a couple of the priestesses making their way behind me to close me in their circle. I extended the dagger in my left hand and drew my sword out of my satchel with my right. It unfolded once freed.

"Take another step and I gut her," I said.

I aimed my sword at Ruith who still writhed on the ground from her bloodied nose. I tossed the dagger in the air and caught its handle. I cocked my arm back as though I was preparing to throw. The double threat called the women up short and they fumbled back, the circle a misshapen scatter-pattern.

"You been holding out on us, Van Alst," said Erwen.

"Let her go," I said pointing at Morgan.

"Why don't you come join us instead?"

"Join a bunch of women who want to violate the autonomy of hundreds of witches, literally robbing them of their power? I don't think so."

"You know, my mother was a psychologist," Erwen said. "She studied matriarchal societies like the Musuo and the Naxi in China. These women handled the business decisions of the society, the political works too. The children took the mothers' last names. Property was passed down to daughters. They had walking marriages where the woman would go to a man's house, take his seed, and raise the child. These societies are peaceful. And do you know why?"

I didn't and I didn't care. Well, except for the walking marriage part. That I wanted to investigate when I had a moment to spare. But right now, I only cared about my cousin. I had to figure out a way to get that spear away from her body.

Looking at Morgan's dark eyes, I could tell she was thinking the same thing. In fact, I felt like I knew that little glint in her eyes. It was the same glint I'd gotten right before I'd clocked Ruith in the nose.

"The reason why is-"

But Erwen didn't have a chance to complete her sentence. Morgan wrenched back and elbowed the high priestess in the gut. The problem with that was that she'd gone low where I'd gone high.

As Erwen stumbled back, the dagger sliced at

Morgan's forearm. The moment the dagger broke her skin, Morgan sunk to the ground.

Erwen took a deep breath. The anger in her sea green eyes burned as though they were on fire. She regained her balance and double-fisted the spear.

Merlin raised his hand towards Erwen. I wasn't sure if it was an attempt to grab Morgan and hold her still or to try and stop Erwen. It was a fleeting motion and he retracted his hand no sooner than he'd raised it.

The blade of the spear glinted in the moonlight. Blood rushed down Morgan's forearm and into the blades of grass. All conscious thought stopped as my emotions consumed me.

I felt a fire burning in my gut. With one deep breath, I stoked the embers and I felt something explode. I was on my feet, moving faster than I ever had before. Faster than I knew a human could move.

My arms reached out and wrapped around Morgan's body. I brought her to me, tasting the salt of her sweat, feeling the slickness of her blood. I held her tight, hugging her body into mine in an effort to protect her from those that would harm us.

But no one was around us.

Merlin, Erwen, the other priestesses, they were

nowhere in sight. Neither was the Tor. Neither was the ground.

We were airborne. I was levitating. Carrying both my weight and Morgan's with the strength of my powers. Like I said, I didn't do anything by halves.

We sailed down the hilltop on a cushion of air. Morgan breathed hard against my cheek. I had to adjust my grip when my palm met the blood still oozing from her arm. And that's when the weight of what I was doing hit me.

Our actual weight. Not only was I carrying myself through the air, I was carrying another living body. My energy stores were quickly depleting.

We sank lower on the horizon, getting closer to the ground. The bottom of the hill was still a bit away. I looked over my shoulder towards the top of the hill. I saw a flurry of robes rushing down the hill.

The sight of the women heading after us, plus the glint of the spear in Erwen's hand, upped my anxiety. Morgan and I sank closer to the ground. If I stuck my feet out, we'd be running.

But from the looks of her, Morgan couldn't run. I had to get us safely down. And then what? I couldn't carry her. An idea splashed into my mind.

"Morgan? Can Viviane hear underwater?"

"I... I don't know?"

Morgan's eyes were closed. Her breathing was getting shallower. Sweat was streaming down her forehead. And the wound at her arm still leaked like a faucet.

I opened my mouth and began shouting for Viviane. I screamed at the top of my lungs as we reached the bottom of the hill. I managed to land us in the Chalice Spring.

I looked down in the waters, relieved to see Viviane peering back at us. She broke the surface and glared at me.

"You got mud all over my boots," she admonished. "Where's the spear?"

"The High Priestess of the Banduri has it," I said ignoring her and stepping into the waters with Morgan. "We need to get Morgan to Gwin. She's been cut by the spear."

**15**

———

Viviane raced us back through the portal. This time the journey was like going on a roller coaster ride. The air pocket made it feel as though we were climbing up and racing down the track at the same time. The energy pummeled my body and roiled my stomach.

I held Morgan tightly in my arms, trying to take the brunt of the motion. She had enough to deal with on her own. Her hands bled all over my shirt to mix with Geraint's tomato stain.

Her body trembled. Her mouth opened, gasping for air. She dry heaved. Then her hacking and wheezing took on a wet, gurgling sound. I leaned her over as she became violently ill.

Hopefully, there was a housekeeper for the ley

lines. Or would Viviane have to come back and clean this up? Or maybe Morgan's upchuck would simply dissolve into the energy and become a part of someone's spell?

I knew I wasn't making any sense. My mind was racing, trying to outrun my fear that Morgan might be losing her magic as Merlin had. But Merlin hadn't been healed after he'd been wounded. His wound was still open, having festered for weeks. Morgan had been hurt moments ago. I just needed to get her back to the castle where she could be healed.

Finally, we broke the surface of the waters with a splash. I looked around to see that we were in the moat of Tintagel castle.

The surrounding grass was wet as though a rain shower had swept the land, but the sky was dark and empty; blameless with no clouds. Somewhere in the distance, a bird chirped, tattle tailing its location so that another might find it. The wind shifted and a pile of leaves fluttered in the air, landing right in front of me.

"She's acting like a mortal," said Viviane as she peered at Morgan. "Humans become sick when they travel by ley line."

Morgan's eyes were pulled closed. Her lips were

fading into a pale blue. Her hand continued to bleed and her body continued to shake with tiny tremors. She wouldn't respond as I shook her and called her name. I tried to stand with her in my arms, but I couldn't. I had no energy left of my own.

"Help," I shouted. But my voice barely carried over the wind. I tried again and again, my voice gaining tenor with each call for help. Until finally, the drawbridge lowered.

The glint of steel, long blades and rounded disks, glinted in the moonlight. When the weapons were lowered, the first face I recognized was Gawain's. His hooded gazed opened wider and wider as he scanned from my head to my toes. It wasn't a long perusal as I was crumbled on the ground with Morgan in my arms.

I breathed a sigh of relief as Gawain dropped his weapons and set his feet in motion towards me. But then he was blocked out by a large mass. In fact, the whole moon was eclipsed from my sight.

"What the hell is going on?" Arthur's voice filled the night sky and shook the tranquility out of the darkness.

I heard a splash behind me as Viviane's pale feet disappeared into the waters. I was left alone with a bleeding witch in my arms. Her blood and magic, and maybe even her life, seeping from her body.

"Help me," I said.

Arthur reached down and swooped Morgan's limp body from my arms. Lifting her as though she were nothing more than a flower plucked from the field. I was actually surprised to see the horror on his face at Morgan's state. I was so used to seeing the two of them go at it with Morgan steaming and Arthur calmly pacifying her. But now his face blanched as he scanned her wound. His stormy gaze fixed on her closed lips that were now nearly as blue as her eyes. He turned with her in his arms and stormed into the castle.

I felt arms pulling me up from the ground. A callused palm tilted up my cheek. Coffee-brown eyes peered into mine and gave me a jolt of energy.

"Can you walk?" Gawain asked.

I could, but I didn't want to be strong any longer. Heroism work was hard, especially when your mission failed. I just wanted to curl into a ball and let someone else take over. My hesitation was all Gawain needed to scoop me up into his arms.

He took over. I rested my head in the crook of his neck and shoulder. Gawain's long strides ate up the distance over the drawbridge as he caught up with Arthur.

Along the way, I saw the squires peering at me. Yuric blew out a long breath and rubbed at his chin as we passed. Maurice scratched the back of his neck while his thick brows wrinkled. A few of the other squires strained to get a glimpse of me as Gawain rushed us inside. I caught sight of Baysle standing apart from the group. His lip curled as he shook his head at me.

I shut my eyes and turned back into Gawain's neck. I could tell when we were inside by the change in temperature. The warmth of the hall lights and wall sconces seeped into my tired bones.

Arthur bellowed for Gwin. His voice was so loud it shook my eyes open. Gwin appeared before us as though she'd materialized out of thin air. I heard her intake of breath deep in my heart as she took in the sight of her sister.

We made it up into the infirmary. The room was blindingly white; white walls, white fixtures, white sheets. Arthur lay Morgan down on one of the cots in the empty room.

He carefully arranged her limbs. Then he brushed her dark hair out of her face. His thumb lingered at the corner of her pale lips. When he straightened, he rounded on me.

"What happened?"

"Merlin," I said. My voice wobbled along with my knees as Gawain set me on my feet.

"Merlin did this?" asked Gwin as she ran her hands over her sister's prone, unresponsive body. "With the Spear of Destiny?"

"No," I said. "He's not the one who sliced her with the spear. It was the High Priestess; Erwen. The one who came to town."

"Where are they? How did they find you?" demanded Arthur.

"They didn't."

I took a deep breath. But when the air expanded in my belly I felt like I was going to throw up. I forced the words to come up first.

"We found them." Then the words kept coming in fast chunks that left a bitter taste as they spilled off my tongue. "Viviane said she knew where Merlin was, and she'd take me to him if I gave her my shoes, and if I used the spear on her to break her curse so she could walk, but she told me not to tell any of you knights because you might cock block us with your chivalry."

Arthur stood sentry at the foot of Morgan's bed.

Gawain and Geraint were posted at the doorway. Gwin chanted over Morgan, who lay prone. Morgan's breathing was labored. The blood continued to pour from her wound. Each bearded face frowned at me in confusion.

"That doesn't make any sense?" said Arthur. "How did we go from shoes to a spear to a witch on the brink of death?"

"I was going to go alone," I said, pushing past the pain in my throat. Though I hadn't vomited any digested food, the words coming out were like acid clawing its way out of my mouth. "Morgan cornered me as I was leaving and I let her talk me into coming along. I thought we'd be okay. I thought we'd save the day and show you..."

My voice sounded like a child's as I trailed off. Show them what? That I was great at being impulsive. Unparalleled in my ability to make rash decisions. A superstar at getting myself into jams. Catlike in my ability to get myself out of danger and land on my feet. Because I was. I'd gotten myself out of this jam completely unscathed.

My eyes went back to Morgan. She still hadn't opened her eyes. She continued to shake and tremble. The bleeding had slowed, but it hadn't stopped.

Gwin's normally calm and dulcet tones held a note of fear as she chanted over her sister.

"I told you to stay here," said Arthur. "I told you to train, to gain the knights' trust. I come back to find two of my knights bruised up from a fall and my squires in a state because they lost not one but two ladies under their protection."

I'd never looked away from a man before. But I did now. I could handle the fury in his eyes. I pissed people off on a regular. What my upset stomach was having trouble digesting was the disappointment woven through his words.

"I'll get my things and go," I said, turning for the door.

"No," said Arthur. "You're not leaving this castle. You'll go to your room and you'll stay there. Someone will guard your door because I can't trust that you'll stay put. That means I need to lose another hand because of you."

Gwin looked up from her vigil over her sister. Her gaze flashed between me and Arthur. She pursed her lips when she looked at me. Then she turned back to her sister and took up her chant.

I turned back to the door. My gaze connected with the two knights standing there. Geraint stood with his back stiff as a straight-edge. Gawain's shoulders were hunched and rounded.

Geraint leaned back, his lip curling down as his accented brows rose in loud judgment.

Gawain lowered his head and pressed his lips together. He avoided my gaze as he made way for me to pass through the door.

No one came to my defense as I left the room. I didn't expect them to. I tried to hold my chin high as I walked, but there was too much weight on my shoulders, and my head hung low.

16

—————

*I*'d never been sent to my room before. I'd never had four permanent walls to call home before. My stay at boarding school was all too brief. My visits to my father's family never felt welcoming. But this room was mine.

The four-poster bed had been my mother's, as was the chest and vanity. Igraine had made the frilly comforter decades ago. The sheet was done in garish pinks that made me think of cough syrup but it kept me warm at night. Gwin had set a vase of flowers on the dresser at the beginning of the week. The blooms were wilting now, but I didn't throw them out.

They were mine. All these things were mine. They'd been given to me to make me feel comfortable and at home. And now all these things could be taken away.

They would be taken away. Because nothing in my life had ever lasted. Not the places I stayed. Not my parents and their loving hugs. Not any of my intimate relationships. Nothing. For some reason, I was like Teflon. Nothing stuck to me.

I wrenched my arms from myself. If they didn't want me here that was fine. I was used to being unwanted. I'd save them the trouble and just bust out of this joint and go where I would be wanted.

My phone slipped out of my clammy palms and I had to bend down to retrieve it. My fingertips were numb as I dialed the number. As it rang and rang, I became more and more anxious. But she picked up on the third ring.

"Hey, girl, heyyy."

My breath caught at the sound of my bestie's voice. Nia sounded happy, chipper. Either she'd dug up some dirt and found an ancient artifact in the bowels of the earth, or she was getting some loving from one of the two men perpetually chasing after her.

One of those guys was a fine ass Frenchman. Zane was an artist who'd been in love with Nia for his entire life; which was a long time since he was also Immortal like her. I loved Zane like a brother. We had a lot in common with art and living a bohemian lifestyle.

But my money was on my bestie's other suitor; billionaire developer, Tresor Mohandis. Did you catch the billionaire part? Tres was a super chic sheik with a brooding alpha attitude. But he had a yacht and a private plane and more money than a girl could count. I was Team Broody Billionaire all the way.

"I was just about to call you," Nia said. "But I didn't want to infringe on your family bonding time. Is Igraine stuffing you with weird parts of animals? Are you even sleeping in your own bed or are you and Gwin and Morgan having slumber parties every night? Wait, first, tell me, does Gawain still have his virtue? Hang on, why are you being so quiet? The only time you're ever quiet is when —What's wrong?"

I opened my mouth now that I could finally get a word in edgewise, and then I choked. It started as a sniffle, and then it became a whimper, and morphed into hiccupping snorts.

"Loren? What? What is it?"

I couldn't answer her. I could only cradle the phone to my face and cry as Nia made cooing noises.

Then she growled through the receiver, demanding to know which knight messed with her girl.

"Was it Gawain? Did he pull that whole I'm facing death BS? Or was it Geraint; the old stick up his arse. Did you put a stick up his arse? Please tell me you didn't put a stick up his arse."

Her repeated use of the word arse got a little chuckle out of me. But the laugh sounded no different from my cries.

"Oh, sweetie, I'm gonna go and charter a plane right now," she said. "I'll be there by tonight."

"No," I finally managed. "Don't do that."

Just the thought that she would come to my aide loosened the pangs in my heart. The fact that she would stick by me was the salve that finally soothed the sick feeling in my gut.

"I'm fine," I said.

That was a lie and I know she knew it. I'd lied to her a fair bit when we'd met, before I got to know her and know that I could trust her.

She'd gotten to know me too. She remained quiet on the other end of the line, waiting patiently for the shoe to drop. Crap. I'd have to tell her that too, that I'd promised her shoes to a water witch.

"I screwed up," I said. "Morgan's hurt and it's all my fault."

For the second time tonight, words spilled from my bowels in a rush. But this time, when I was finished, I felt relieved. At the same time, I wished my best friend was here with me because I needed a hug. But she was on the other side of the world. And she remained mute.

"I was trying to help," I said in my defense. "These knights are not giving me a chance. I was trying to prove myself."

I waited in the silence. I heard her inhale, and then her sigh. I huffed.

"Obviously, you have an opinion on the matter," I said. "Go on."

"Okay, sweetie," she said. "Do you want me to talk smack about Artie and his merry boy band? Or do you want me to tell you the big-girl's-panties truth?"

"Nia," I groaned. "You know I hate underwear."

"Yeah, I do know that. I've just bought a whole new wardrobe because of it."

I had a habit of borrowing her clothes and going commando. "How about this? Can we avoid the ugly truth and you just come back here and get me?"

Nia took a deep, audible breath. On the exhale, she said the one word I didn't want to hear. "No."

I flopped back on the bed. "Puh-lease." I pressed the phone between my chin and shoulder and threw my arms out. Tossing my head from side to side, I kicked my heels at the edge of the mattress.

"No," Nia said more firmly. "You're going to go downstairs and make nice with the others. You're going to share your lunch. You're not going to toss sand in the sandbox. You're going to stay there and fix this, Loren. These people are your family."

"You're my family."

"Which is why I'm doling out the tough love."

I sat up on the bed, folding my legs under me. "You wouldn't have done the same thing?"

"Hell yeah, I would've," she said. "And I would've been just as wrong as you are now. Remember, the last time I did something stupid? You almost died."

Of course, she'd throw that in my face. Poor Morgan was laid up in the infirmary, likely losing her magic, possibly losing her life.

"You and I both have a habit of running away from our pasts," said Nia. "I'm there with you —in spirit. Cause I'm on the other side of the world and all. But you have to do this. You have to see it through. If you don't you'll hate yourself."

She was wrong. I already hated myself. But she was also right. No one had asked me to leave. No one had turned me out. If I left it was on me.

"But let Artie know that I will charter a plane and kick his Celtic ass if he makes you cry again."

"I can't do that," I said. "I can't leave my room."

There was a brief pause in which I could feel her surprise. "Wow, so they actually went medieval on your ass."

**17**

———

*I* didn't go march anywhere after I got off the phone with Nia. No, I did what all guilty people did; I rested inside my cell and plotted my next move. After a long, fitful night's sleep of tossing and turning, I'd made my decision.

I put my friend's boots on, strapped my father's bag over my shoulder, and opened the bedroom window. Hefting myself over the ledge, I got a foothold on the bricks of the castle.

It was an easy maneuver. I was an avid rock climber. These old castle walls with their nooks and crannies were nothing to a seasoned climber like me.

Making my way over to the next room, I jimmied

open the window, and slipped inside. It was Morgan's bedroom.

She had a TARDIS blue comforter spread over her bed. Instead of celebrities or models, posters of the Periodic Table and old white men with messy hair and frantic eyes were displayed on her wall. I recognized Einstein and assumed the other old-world pocket protectors were also great men of science. There was a stack of textbooks whose names I couldn't hope to pronounce, even though I spoke a couple of languages passably and had been drilled in Latin since I was a child. There was also a letter from Cambridge University.

I ran my fingers over the embossed lettering of the old institution. My forefinger tracked down to a single word; accepted. Then I noted, it wasn't the only acceptance letter. There was a stack of them. From Harvard, Yale, the University of Dubai. All over the world, institutions of higher learning wanted Morgan on their roster. But she was stuck here, her magic and skills at the exclusive beck and call of her community. And now, thanks to me, she might not leave that sick bed.

When I opened Morgan's bedroom door there was a mountain in my way. Maurice's large body sat back against my door. His eyes were closed, his mouth open as he snored softly.

I climbed over my night guard and began down the hall. But then I stopped and turned back. I leaned down and gave the kid a shake.

Maurice woke with a start. His first instinct was to offer me a friendly smile. Then his brow furrowed as realization slowly dawned. He looked over his shoulder at the closed door to my room and then back to me. In a matter of five seconds, his face went from friendly, to confusion, to betrayal.

"Look," I said, straightening and holding my hands in surrender. "I'm not escaping. I just want to go and check on Morgan."

"Oh." Maurice blinked. His features relaxed into something soft and accepting. "You could've asked, you know?"

I nodded, but I didn't know. "I'll be back, okay?"

He smiled, then he closed his eyes and leaned his back against my door frame. He was softly snoring again in a second as though he didn't have a care in the world. As though he trusted that I would keep my word and return.

I took a deep breath and made my way to the infirmary. Outside the door to the infirmary stood another roadblock.

Unlike Maurice, Gawain was wide awake as he leaned against the infirmary's door. I didn't startle him as I approached. He looked as though he'd been waiting for my arrival.

"There's been no change," said Gawain. "She hasn't woken up."

"I didn't mean for any of this to happen."

"I believe you."

Unable to meet his gaze, I looked down at his boots. They were cowboy boots. It was the most mashed up fashion statement I'd seen thus far in this town. An Asian male with his torso covered in a medieval tunic, his thighs poured into dark leather pants that screamed metal band, and his feet stuffed into cowboy boots.

"No one here is your enemy, Loren."

I huffed a laugh. "Did Geraint and Baysle get that memo?"

"They're waiting for any evidence that you trust us."

My gaze jerked to his then. Both of those men had accused me of stealing, of lying, and cheating. Okay, all which I had done.

"The people in this town have reached out their hands to you and you still have your arms crossed over your chest. And, yeah, Gerry can be an asshole at times. This is his family. He'd die to protect anyone in this town. We all would."

So I'd walked into a cult. A magical mafia where if you messed with one, you messed with all. I had that with Nia. She'd risked her life for me and I'd done the same for her. But I couldn't imagine having a couple hundred besties. It sounded overwhelming.

I wrapped my arms around myself, squeezing myself tight. But then I noted that my arms were more muscled than my workouts afforded me. My arms also reached all the way around my back and were able to squeeze the opposite shoulders.

Those weren't my arms. They were Gawain's. He wrapped me up in a tight bear hug that I couldn't escape. I simply had to take the smothering affection.

"I'd die for you," he said. "I think you're worth it."

"If you think I'm worth it now, standing and fully clothed, wait until you get me horizontal and naked."

Gawain chuckled. His laugh rumbled through me and I rubbed my cheek against the opening of his shirt until I found skin.

"I know we've only known each other a short time," Gawain said, pulling away from me. "But I can't imagine not having you as a friend."

I cocked my head to the side as I peered up at his

handsome face. He smiled, but there was no flirty tilt to those lips. His gaze was soft but serious.

"You are totally friend-zoning me, aren't you?"

"No." He gave a shake of his head. "I'm welcoming you into my family."

"Like, as your sister?"

"I..." That caught him up short. Then he shrugged. "Call it what you want, but it would've never worked out between us. Face it; you were only into my body."

Now I snorted. Though the man did have a good point. A very good point I thought as I eyed his chest.

"I have a lot more to offer," Gawain insisted.

"Yeah, you have really good pecs —I mean personality—too."

Gawain's grin reflected in his eyes. The spark of desire that had been there was doused, but it was still there. I wasn't sure if I'd hold still in the friendly place he'd just put me. But I could hang out for a while.

"Go on inside, Loren. I'm sure it'll help Morgan to hear your voice. Let her know her family's here for her."

Gawain let me go and headed down the hall. I turned my attention back to the closed door, took a deep breath, and opened it. The first thing I saw was Gwin tightening Morgan's sheets.

Morgan lay with her dark hair spread out on the white pillow. Her skin was pale enough to match the sheets her sister tucked around her shoulders. But at least her lips weren't blue anymore. The forearm, which had been struck by the spear, was now bandaged. It looked as though Gwin had gotten the bleeding under control. Morgan's breathing was even. But her eyes remained closed.

I hadn't been allowed in the room when my mother had died, but I'd snuck in. Her face had been pale, paler than Morgan's. Her blonde hair had turned from vibrant to dull. Her eyes had never opened again after that night.

I shook myself to let go of that memory. The door to the sick room slipped out of my fingers and closed with a soft snick. Gwin looked up and saw me. I averted my gaze from hers. My body turned towards the door when I heard her steps coming closer to me.

Nia's voice rang in my ear. Big girl panties time. I braced for impact. A good thing because I was nearly knocked over by Gwin's embrace.

"I'm so sorry, Loren. In the chaos of last night, I didn't check to make sure you were unharmed." She took my hands in hers, running her fingers over my arms and then my face.

"I'm fine."

Gwin stared at me with eyes so like my mother's that the truth slipped out.

"Physically."

Gwin nodded, her blue eyes soft with sympathy. "We're all going to get through this."

My eyebrows felt heavy as they crinkled, squinting at her in utter confusion. "You're not angry with me because of what happened to your sister?"

"I'm furious with you both," she growled.

I tried to pull my hands away but Gwin didn't let go.

"Are you sure you're okay?" she asked, but didn't wait for my response. "I'll get you something to eat. Igraine made your favorite."

"She did?"

"Of course, she did. It's all for you. No one else will eat that garbage."

I took a deep breath, trying to hold myself still. Everything in me wanted to run away. My heart was beating so fast I'm sure Gwin could feel my pulse pushing against her fingers as she held onto my hands. Her eyes were soft as she continued to check me over, much like Maurice's had been when he realized I wasn't trying to escape. Her hold was comforting like Gawain's. My shoulders slumped as all the fight went out of me.

I looked over at Morgan. I wished she'd sit up and crack a joke. But she remained prone.

I hadn't noticed it before, but now standing nearer to her, I noted that Morgan felt different. She'd always felt so full of energy, like being near a live wire. But now she felt hollow, empty, human. What if all her magic was gone?

"She's going to be okay?" My voice trembled as I asked.

"She's going to be okay." Gwin's face was determined, but I heard the note of uncertainty in her voice.

I couldn't stand still any longer. I had to get out of the room. "You stay here," I said. "I'll go down to the kitchen and grab a bite."

But I didn't go down to the kitchen. I walked slowly down the steps and stood outside the door to the Throne Room. I raised my hand and knocked.

Tristan opened the door. When he saw me he winced in the universal language that said everyone was talking about me behind my back.

"Lady Loren," Arthur's booming voice carried

into the hall. "I thought I asked you to stay in your room."

"You ordered it, my lord. And I did. Now I'd like to say something, if I may?"

I slipped past Tristan and made my way inside. All six knights were assembled, each man in the seat of his ancestor. I walked up to my grandfather's seat, but I didn't sit down. I stood behind the seat, which was exactly across from Arthur.

"Okay. So here goes." I took a deep breath and did something I hadn't done in a long time. I spoke my heart's desire out loud. "I want this; this seat. And I'm not very good at wanting things. I'm used to getting them, to taking them, to faking things. But I can't take this. I can't fake it."

I squeezed the back of the chair. My gaze caught Gawain's. His dark eyes were encouraging as they rested on me.

"It's always just been me and my mum," I continued. "Then me and my dad. Then more recently, me and my bestie. I don't know how to do the group thing —and anyone who'd tell you differently, just know I had to have been really drunk that night."

No laughs. I bit my lower lip. Tough room.

"Okay, look. I don't know how to be a family. I was just getting the hang of a partnership. But I've been a fighter all my life." I took another deep breath and dug deep for words to make these guys hear me out. "Life can be a challenge. Life can seem impossible. It's never easy when there's so much on the line. But you and I can make a difference. There's a mission just for you and me."

Geraint cocked his head to the side and glowered at me. "Isn't that from the *Pokemon Movie*?"

"Only the last little bit," I snapped. "I got lost and I didn't know how to end it. Let me try again."

"That's enough, Lady Loren," said Arthur.

My heart sank. My nails dug into the top of my grandfather's seat leaving behind half-moon crescents. He was going to do it. He was going to kick me out. I'd pushed too far. This is why I hated reaching for things.

"Decisions like these," Arthur began, "decisions that affect all of us, are decided by consensus. We were just about to vote when you interrupted."

My head jerked up. It wasn't over? I still had a chance? But then my gaze latched on Geraint. Between the quirk in his accented brows and the smug lift of his mouth, I knew what his vote would be.

"My vote is no," he said. "I still say a woman can't be a knight."

"Surprise, surprise," I mumbled.

"That's not sexist," Geraint said. "Women are equal in 99% of things. Rushing into battle is the one thing I won't make a concession on. I don't get why that makes me a bad guy?"

He looked around the room. I did too, but I couldn't read any of the male faces around the table. Maybe it was because too much hair covered their features.

"I've seen our lady in battle," said Lancelot. "She proved that she can take on combat operations when we were in Mosul. She's physically capable, mentally capable."

I had to hold myself still before I rushed over to give the ginger-haired feminist a hug. But I'm glad I held still because Lance wasn't finished.

"It's her morals that worry me," he continued. "I can't trust that she'll always do the right thing. So my vote is no. I'm sorry, my lady."

I stood stunned. My palms pressed into the back of the chair trying to keep my body upright from the impact of the sucker punch. Percival was next and I had no idea which way he'd sway the count.

Percival stroked the whiskers on his beard. His irises appeared to bounce around in his eye socket like his mind was working fast inside his skull and he couldn't quite keep up. When he spoke, it was slow and thoughtful.

"Being that she is a woman, she has a particular skill set which means an increase in the talent pool. She can take on missions that we can't. That will up our odds of success. My vote is yes."

I let out a gush of air I hadn't known I'd been holding. Two to one. Three left. I turned to Tristan who was next.

"Recruitment is at an all-time low." The young man's eyes were thoughtful as he spoke. "We need to allow the mixing of the genders if we are to keep our ranks up. And we need to get with the modern times. Our way of life is dying out. We need to evolve. I vote yes."

I balled my hand into a fist and did a covert victory pump behind my grandfather's chair. It was nearly mine. That was two yeses and two nos.

I knew Gawain would vote for me. With all the sexual tension between us over the past few weeks, and that lame we-are-family talk earlier was just a ploy. He so wanted me. He was likely making sure we were covering our basis before everyone found out we were cavorting coworkers.

"My vote is no."

I leaned over the chair, turning my ear to him to

make sure I heard him correctly this time. "I'm sorry, what?"

Gawain looked up at me from beneath that hooded gaze. "I've seen men act foolishly to protect a woman. I know that Lady Loren is talented, probably more than some of us. But I think her inclusion will affect the cohesion of our order. My vote is no."

Gawain took a deep breath. He exhaled it slowly, then his gaze tracked up to mine. He folded his hands in front of him on the table and leaned forward.

I leaned back. I let go of the seat. My palms felt damp. My fingertips were numb.

That was three nos and two yeses. I turned to Arthur. I didn't know if he would create a tie or if my fate was already sealed with Gawain's betrayal.

Once again, Arthur's steely gaze pinned me in place. Never had I wanted to run more than in that moment. I knew my fate before he spoke it.

"I did not like the idea of a female knight when it was first presented to us. There is an order to our way of life. The standards of physical fitness for our order is suited to men and I've always believed it would over-stretch and overtax a woman. I didn't think a woman had the longevity or the physiology or the emotional stamina to undertake this life."

I curled my hands into a fist instead of rushing to wrap my hands around his neck to stave off his pigheaded words. The only reason I didn't lunge was because I heard a *but* in his speech. I held my breath as he got there.

"You've proven me wrong. *But*...I do not think you're ready, my lady. I don't trust my life in your hands. I still feel that I can't turn my back and know you'll have it."

He held my gaze. My eyes burned but I refused to let a tear fall. I just wanted him to get on with it, to just say it so that I could get out of here.

"My vote is; no."

I nodded once. Holding my head high, I walked to the door. I shut it quietly behind me and headed out of the castle doors.

## 18

——————

$\mathcal{I}$ walked out into the crisp evening air. The sun was setting, slowly tucking itself into the horizon for the night. The few trickle of tourists had left the grounds as the attractions closed at 5 pm. Most, if not all, of the town's people were inside the Great Hall, sitting down for the nightly community dinner. I'd lost my appetite.

That was a lie.

I could eat. I just couldn't stomach walking into that room full of people as a failure.

I closed my eyes, shutting out this magical world. But the loss of sight didn't help. The magic was inside me.

I wanted to run across the drawbridge. I wanted

to hightail it out of this town. I wanted to escape back to my life of transience. But I couldn't move.

My feet felt rooted. My gut felt settled. My heart felt heavy, but not sad heavy. The weight in my chest felt like it was tethered.

I walked to the middle of the bridge and sat down. The toe of my boot tapped the water. I watched the ripples spread from the point of my boot on out to the water's edge. It hit the brick of the castle on one end and the paved path that led into the town on the other.

I looked from one side to the other as the ripples settled and the waters stilled once more. Once the waters calmed, I was left with my reflection. A pair of eyes stared back at me but they weren't my own.

"Hey, Viviane."

The witch's face materialized out of the water. As she rose, the droplets fell from her ivory hair as though the surface of the water was a magical blow dryer. Her tresses came to rest in lush waves around her shoulders. Women would kill for a manufactured device that could perform that trick.

"I liked it when you called me Vivi," she said. "No one's ever given me a nickname. Mostly, they just shout at me when they need a transport. Or if their shoe has gone missing."

She reached over and ran a finger over my boots. I yanked them away. "Maybe I'd keep calling you by a nickname if you stick around. You totally bailed on me last night."

She sunk back into the water until only her eyes were visible. They were huge, somber orbs that reflected the moon on the surface of the waters.

"Did The Arthur shout at you?" she asked.

It took me a moment before I responded as I puzzled over how she spoke out loud while her mouth was submerged in the waters. "No. He didn't shout. Which made it all the worse. I prefer the shouting to the quiet disappointment."

Viviane rose up from the waters again. She rested her elbows on the drawbridge. I saw her lame feet dangling listlessly in the moat. "He was disappointed that you didn't catch Merlin and you nearly got Morgan killed?"

I turned and glared at her. She was as culpable as me. But her gaze was fixed on her forfeited prize. "No, he's disappointed that I went off and did those things without him or the other knights. They expect instant trust. But trust is a two-way street."

"I've never walked on a street."

"Me neither," I sighed. "Metaphorically speaking."

"I was speaking physically."

My glare softened as I regarded her. Viviane rested her pale head on her arms. They were surprisingly slender, like the rest of her. I wondered that they held her up.

"Are there others like you?" I asked. "Mermaids or sirens?"

"They're not what you expect. They're not human and they're not nice. I'm not exactly like them. I'm not entirely like you." She rubbed her nose into the crook of her elbow. "Anyway, it was a stupid idea, trying to get the spear, thinking I could break this curse, imagining I could walk. I'm sorry I dragged you into it. I'm sorry Lady Morgan got hurt."

She released her hold on the bridge and sank back down into the water.

"Viviane, wait," I called out. "Vivi?"

She broke the water, a small smile on her lips, a glimmer of hope in her eyes. It was the ray of hope that did me in. That single ray tugged at the tether on my heartstrings, pulling me closer to her.

"It wasn't a stupid idea," I said, leaning down towards her. "We just went about it the wrong way."

"Should we go back to the Tor?" she asked.

"No," I said. "The knights already went back and searched the hill. Merlin and the Banduri were long gone. But going it alone, that's the wrong way. God, I sound like an *After School Special*."

"I didn't go to school."

"Trust me, you're better for it. But here's the lesson I think we're supposed to learn."

Viviane tread in the moonlit water. The night critters paused in their leg rubbing and croaking. The wind hushed its whispers and left the night silent for a moment. All awaited my sage soliloquy.

"Actually, I'm not a hundred percent certain of the moral to this story. But I'm pretty sure it has to do with community, and working together, and trust. Because that's what we got wrong the first time. We should've called for backup."

Vivi nodded enthusiastically. But I got the feeling she didn't know what I was talking about any more than I did. What I did know was that I wasn't leaving this place. At least not yet.

I'd done a scary thing back in the Throne Room. I'd let down my guard and let those men see me vulnerable. And they'd rejected me. But I hadn't died.

Most of the knights saw that I had what it took to stand next to them. They just needed to trust me enough to stand behind them as well as beside them. I just had to prove to them that I would make the right decisions when push came to shove.

And since well-thought out, impeccably-researched, scientifically-logical decisions were not my forte, I was probably screwed.

I turned back to Vivi. Her eager expression reminded me of Morgan's when she begged me to go hunt Merlin. "Vivi? Are you sure that spear will cure you? It stripped Merlin of his power. And Morgan... she hasn't woken up yet."

Vivi's expression turned somber. "This isn't magic I want to have. If the spear will break the binds, I will throw myself upon it."

I still wasn't convinced. The feeling of being near Morgan's barren body, and Merlin's hollow cavity sent a shiver down my spine. "Maybe we could do magic shoes like in *The Wizard of Oz*."

"I don't know of any place called Oz? Is it on the ley line?"

Before I could answer, the ground rumbled. I heard a splinter from one of the wooden slats of the drawbridge.

"What was that?" I asked.

"There's something dark coming." In the waters, Vivi wrapped her arms around her frame. "All I can see is black and blue."

I stood. Off in the distance, coming up the streets that led from the town, I saw a crowd of figures moving towards us. The bodies were all tall, hourglass shapes indicating that they were women. Their forms were all draped in flowing fabric that shimmered in the moonlight. Even from this distance, I could make out her red hair.

Erwen led a group of two dozen Banduri down the street towards the castle. They walked up the hill. Dozens and dozens of women. It was like a suffragette march. Moving slowly behind her was Merlin. He looked even worse for the wear. Sickness swirled in my gut as they moved closer and I saw something even more awful.

In their hands, they each held a rock. A large, blue rock. Bluestones.

"Do not worry," said Viviane. "They cannot breach the shield."

The shield? I turned and looked up at the castle. It shone brightly in the moonlight. I didn't need to blink to shift my view from magical to human. I saw it as clear as if it were day and I was mortal.

"Morgan," I breathed. "Morgan isn't helping to hold the shield any longer. We're all vulnerable. Camelot is under attack."

## 19

"We have to warn everyone," I said hopping up. But when I looked down it was only to see my reflection in the water. Only a tiny swirl remained in the otherwise calm waters, like the last dregs going down a drain. Viviane had deserted me yet again.

So, I was zero for two with my inspirational, team rallying speeches tonight.

No matter. Still, I knew I couldn't embark on this quest alone. Backup was a must this time. I ran back across the drawbridge shouting as I went.

"Raise the drawbridge," I shouted as I felt the sickening heat of the bluestones held in the priestesses' hands.

Baysle poked his head out through one of the

gaps of the battlements as I made my way up to the gatehouse. I saw fluorescent lights flickering in the palm of his hands. For a moment, I wondered if he had hidden talents of a wizard. Then I heard the *bleeping* and *blooping* of a video game and realized it was a handheld device.

Boys were the same no matter their environment. Even when the opportunity to fight a real-life battle presented itself, they still kept their gaze fixed on a screen preferring to fight a fictitious battle of pixels.

Baysle sneered at me, raising one eyebrow in a near perfect mimic of his sire. "What have you done now?"

"We're under attack."

"That's impossible. Camelot's never been under a-"

Baysle's smirk faded when he lowered his gaming device and looked out at the horizon. The Banduri had made it past the sword in stone attraction and were headed toward the lowered drawbridge. But then he squinted his eyes and his face relaxed.

"Those are just a bunch of human women," he huffed.

I didn't have the time or the patience to deal with a kid's ignorance. Unfortunately, he was bigger than me and his bulk was blocking the doorway to the gate's entrance. His eyes narrowed at me as if he knew what I was planning. He crossed his arms over his chest and puffed up his chest, making himself bigger.

My first instinct was to go for his most vulnerable parts. But he was still a kid, and he was technically a part of the group I was trying to protect. Which meant kicking him in his jewels would be counterproductive to my end goal.

But I still needed to get this big oaf out of my way. If booted force wouldn't do it, I'd just have to use another skill. Taking a deep breath, I focused on the anger boiling in my gut.

I took a few steps back. Baysle proved he had a few more brain cells than I expected when he frowned at me instead of smiling in triumph. I crouched like a track runner. Counting in my head, I took off, launching my body up and over Baysle's head.

This time, I only had my weight to deal with on the takeoff and the flight. The landing was a different story. I tucked and rolled as I shot into the gatehouse. Having no brakes, I came to a dead stop on my ass. Thank God there was no one there to see it.

Shooting to my feet, I reached for the lever to raise the drawbridge. It seemed like forever before I heard the cranking of the gears to lift the bridge. But by then it was too late.

I looked down out the glass-less window to see that the priestesses were already filing around the inner rim of the moat. I knew in my soul that something bad would happen if they completed a circle.

I opened my mouth to begin shouting for the knights to take up arms. But then I saw that there was an intercom. I pushed the red button.

"Grab your shining armor boys and get moving. We're under attack."

I shoved my way past Baysle, who still stared dumbfounded down at the women encroaching the boundaries of the castle. Before I'd even gotten back down to the bottom of the guard tower, men were filing out of the castle doors.

Their swords and shields were raised. Then those same weapons lowered when they got an eyeful of their opponents.

"They're women," said Percival.

"It's them," I said. "The Banduri, the ones who hurt Morgan. Merlin's with them. They have the spear."

Six bearded jaws crinkled in confusion as they

looked out at the feminine bodies preparing to face off against them.

"What are we supposed to do?" said Geraint. "We can't fight women. We're knights."

"You don't have to fight them," I said. "Just don't let them form a circle with the stones. It'll weaken our magic and the protections over the castle."

Already, they were halfway around the base of the castle. It should take the two dozen women just a couple of minutes to make their way around the entire structure. Which in theory, would mean they could be easily blocked or diverted or stopped before they met in the middle.

In theory.

If you added to that theory a half dozen battle-hardened, large men with swords and shields intent on protecting their turf, it should be an impossible task for those women to join in the middle and complete said circle.

In theory.

However, a major stipulation in the theory involved men who took an oath to never do harm to any woman. So, the results were a failure. In fact, the results were a comedy of errors.

Percival blocked the path of one of the priestesses. But his blocking looked like a bad football play. She dodged right and he followed. She faked left and, when he went to follow he kept his hands out to the sides instead of grabbing at her. With his hands out to the sides, he lost his balance and fumbled, falling to his knees. She slipped around him. Percy shot up, ready to head after her, only to be confronted with the next priestess in the lineup. And the exact same play repeated.

On the other end of the field, Tristan was faced off with two priestesses. One got around him. Unlike Percy, the younger knight did reach out. And when he did, his hands landed on the woman's boob.

She gasped, outraged.

Tristan pulled back his hand and apologized profusely, only to have his nose get a pummeling. I knew the direct hit didn't hurt him. But the kid stood there flummoxed. He held up his hands, as though completely unwilling to make another move against the women.

This was not going well.

As I watched the priestesses evade the knights, I got a sick feeling in my belly. My head fogged and my eyes watered. Wiping away a tear, I looked up to see Erwen approaching me, a huge blue rock in her hand.

Everything in me told me to take a step back. But I didn't. I held my ground and faced my nemesis.

"Don't try to play hero, Van Ass. We all know where that always gets you. You on your ass with your friends hurt."

"Why are you so mean? Did your mother not give you hugs as a kid?"

"No, she didn't. She did a study that showed hugging and social bonding produce aberrant emotional responses in children."

"That clears up so much," I said. "Then let me approach this logically. These knights and those witches have been protecting the world from some really ugly stuff for centuries — millennia. There are things on this planet that will eat your soul and drink your bones. I've seen it with my own eyes. Did you ever consider that this power was given to us by Mother Nature to protect humanity?"

"Of course, I considered that."

"Oh. And?"

Erwen shrugged. "Doesn't change the fact that you have something that doesn't belong to you. Now it's time to give it back."

Erwen held up the rock. She opened her mouth. I took a moment to note that her lipgloss color was Ruby Roo Retro Matte from MAC. Erwen pursed her lips and blew. A cloud of blue dust blinded my eyes and choked my airways.

I felt myself falling. It seemed to take forever for me to hit the ground. The last thing I remembered was that I seriously had to give up on my attempts at these inspirational speeches.

## 20

When I opened my eyes, my head was foggy. My ass hurt. My body was being dragged.

I felt strong arms come underneath me and drag me up and away. I looked up into the stern face of Geraint.

For a moment, my brain protested. I was certain he was dragging me to Erwen to give me as ransom. But he dragged me back towards the castle doors.

"That was stupid," he said.

"Stupid? Ballsy? I have trouble distinguishing the two."

"We don't have time for jokes," he said. "Get on your feet. We need every man."

I played his words back in my head and then my face split into a grin. "Did you just call me a man?"

That had to be high praise coming from him.

"I'm sure you'll do something even stupider to make me eat those words shortly." Geraint handed the blunt end of my grandfather's sword to me. It was an olive branch. With a sharp point.

I took it from him and we both turned back towards the fray. My joy from the tiny bonding moment was short-lived. Priestesses lined the front of the castle grounds. I couldn't see behind the castle, but I knew that the priestesses had completed their circle. Mainly because all the knights were standing in a cluster at the entryway as the last line of defense.

Everyone in town was inside the castle. Well, actually they were all piled into the Great Hall, peering out through windows and doorways. I saw faces young and old standing defiantly, ready to do whatever was necessary to protect their own.

I turned away from the witches and looked towards the knights. Lance and Gawain stood at the forefront. Tristan, Percival, and Geraint moved to join them. I made ready to stand with them, but I felt a hand hold me back.

"Stay here," said Arthur.

"I can help."

"I know. You need to stay and protect the people. No one gets past this line. Can I trust you?"

Once again, he peered at me with those steel gray eyes. No speech. Just a question.

I knew it was a test. I knew the correct answer that would grant me high marks. But it wasn't the test I wanted to take. I wanted the final exam, the one that would mark me as a knight, the one where I got to save the day from the frontlines and not from the sidelines.

Nodding my head in agreement made me more nauseous than when Erwen had blown the blue powder in my face. But I did it. Then I stepped back and let the men go ahead of me.

Gwin stood in the doorway to the castle. I saw her lips moving in a chant. I felt the air thickening as it did when she opened a ley line. But where there would be a strong wind coming from a ley door, there was only a whisper now.

Stress and strain were clear on Gwin's brow. Her neck was damp with sweat. Tears streamed from her blue eyes. Her shoulders slumped as though a heavy weight was deposited on her entire body.

"I can't hold it," she panted. "The stones are making me weak."

"Here let me help you, child." Igraine came out of the castle and put her hands on Gwin's shoulder.

Gwin and Igraine held hands. Their lips moved in sync as they chanted. I couldn't hear the words, but I felt them in the pit of my stomach. I felt the magic that surrounded the castle ebbing and flowing like the tide. But the tide was low as those bluestones worked against them.

More women left the safety of the castle. They linked hands and stood side by side, back to back with Gwin and Igraine. Their lips moved in sync, picking up the chant to strengthen the protective charm. Deep inside, I knew their collective powers wouldn't be enough to hold back the carcinogenic effects of the blue kryptonite.

The children came next. Young witches from teens to adolescents filled in the gaps between the adult women. Their high-pitched voices joined together to defend the ones who'd taken care of them all their lives.

And then there was me. Standing in front of them with my grandfather's sword in my hand. But when I looked down, the weapon had slipped out of my hand. My feet moved on their own towards Gwin. I took my cousin's hand in mine. I didn't know what I was doing. I didn't know how to shield.

"The magic is inside you," said Igraine. "In your gut, in your heart."

The sounds of the children's voices filled my ears. The sight of Igraine on one side of me and the dressmaker, Minerva, on the other side of me, and the knights making a barrier in front of all of us; that sight overwhelmed me. I shut my eyes and the magic surged up from my gut and pounded in my heart. I gripped Gwin's hand as it poured out of my body, so fast that I couldn't control it. I just opened myself up, willing to do whatever was necessary to protect these people, my family.

The magic in me knew how to protect the things it held dear. I felt it flooding out of me and around everyone in this town. When I opened my eyes again, I saw the protective shield extending beyond the people, beyond the knights, beyond the castle and pushing its way towards the waters surrounding it. It met resistance at the edge of the waters where I knew the priestesses were standing with their stones.

My magic mixed with that of everyone in the town and it shoved at the blue toxin. I felt the spirit, the soul of every person all from Gwin's strong heartbeat to Igraine's firm hand to the children's glowing souls.

With one last push, the power surged through me. There was an explosion of energy from the untouched well inside of me. Then there was an explosion outside of me. I looked out towards the moat and saw blue dust spilling into the air and falling to the ground. One by one, the bluestones exploded.

Like I said, I didn't know how to be subtle.

Cheers went up from the people of the town. I felt myself being embraced inside the oversized cocoon of protection that I had made. All around, I felt arms embracing me. Kids hugged my legs, adults wrapped their arms around my waist, my shoulders.

So, this is what heroism felt like. I kinda hoped we got invaded on a weekly basis because euphoria was the best mind-altering substance I'd ever come into contact with.

Finally, I noticed that there weren't many male voices mixed in with the cheering. I looked to where I'd last seen the knights. They all had their backs to me. Had they even seen my awesome feat? Why weren't they cheering my heroism?

I huffed as I glared at their backsides. Then I noticed that the men were no longer fanned out. They were all clustered at one point, pushing at the invisible shield.

Lance tried to slice the air with his sword, but the tip screeched against the void like nails on a chalkboard. Gawain thrust his shield at the same space and jerked his arm away in pain. My heart stopped when I saw the reason they were trying to break free of my protection.

Arthur was on the outside. Erwen stood before him. The Spear of Destiny was lowered to his neck.

21

_______

*I* left the embracing and cheering and made my way over to the knights. I reached down and picked up my sword where I'd dropped it. The magic in my veins hummed at my fingertips like a livewire as I walked over to the edge of the protective shield.

"What have you done?" Lance demanded. "We can't get out."

"Loren, you have to undo it," said Gawain.

But I didn't know how. So far all I'd been able to do with magic was make things go boom. I didn't know how to reel it back in.

"Loren, don't do anything but what you were told," said Arthur from the other side of the invisible shield. "Keep the shield up. Protect the people."

The man stood proud in the face of a weapon that would rend him mutilated at best, dead at worst. He stared down at Erwen who, although tall, barely came up to Arthur's shoulder. Her sea green eyes were wild with triumph at her great catch.

The other priestesses clustered in a huddle. Their circle was broken. Their one and only weapon against magic had turned to dust, though the blue powder was sprinkled all over their faces and robes like they were coming from a fairy-dusted rave.

Ruith stood beside Merlin with her kohl on the good eye to match the eye I'd blackened. It worked for her. What can I say, she did sinister well.

Merlin looked the worst for the wear. His body was hunched over. It looked as though he'd lost a good clump of the gray hair that had barely covered his head.

My gaze went back to Arthur. Would this be the great warrior's fate once Erwen sliced and diced him with that spear?

"Erwen, Merly's not looking so great." Thalia came up to stand beside a hunched Merlin. "I think he might need a doctor."

"He doesn't need a doctor, you nit," said Ruith. "He's dying.

"And his brother is about to join him," said Erwen.

"Oh, no," said Thalia. "No, no, no. I'm not comfortable with killing. We voted; cure, not kill."

Thalia turned around to face the other priestesses. Not a single one of them had the same wildfire in their eyes as Erwen and Ruith. But neither did a single one of them speak up.

Merlin's spine straightened slightly as his gaze locked with his brother's. I didn't have a sibling so I didn't understand the silent communication that passed between the two men.

It didn't matter. There wasn't anything that Merlin could do. There wasn't anything that any of us could do. Because of me.

I raised my hand to pound against the wall of a mess that I'd created. But unlike Lance who'd met a solid obstruction, my hand went straight through. In fact, my whole body went through. I'd packed a good bit of force into my angry fist and, when I didn't meet any resistance, I stumbled through.

My feet did a couple hop steps. My arms windmilled as I fought to keep my balance. And praise all that was holy, I stayed on my feet and didn't land on my ass when I came face to face with my adolescent tormentors.

I had the urge to do that heel-click-arm-raise thing did gymnasts did at the end of their routine. I certainly had everyone's attentions on me after my little performance. But no one was happy at my arrival.

Behind me, the knights pushed and pressed and tried to shoulder their way out of the shield. But there was no give. I suppose since it was my magic, I could pass through it.

And so here I was, on the wrong side of a barrier, with my arch nemesis, who had a weapon of mass destruction angled at the strongest man I knew. All I could think was one thing...

It was hero time!

I just needed to figure out how to save the day.

"Loren, go back inside," commanded Arthur. "That's an order."

His hands were down. His shoulders tensed. His brows bunched in concentration as he bore into Erwen. I didn't see how she could stand his steely glare.

"I would follow your command," I said. "But unfortunately, you're not the boss of me."

"The people need you to hold the shield."

True. But they needed Arthur as their leader. These people had embraced me, literally. But they'd thrived before me and they would after me. Together, with all their collective energy focused, they could hold that shield. I was an anomaly, an outsider. Again, literally.

I stood apart from the town, apart from the knights, apart from the villainous clique. But I knew what I had to do.

I turned to Erwen. "You want to get rid of magic, right? Well, he has little compared to me. I'm full of it."

"You are full of it, Van Ass," hissed Ruith.

"Oh, grow up and listen to someone with common sense, and a far superior fashion sense than you. That shield won't last long, and when it does come down, chivalry will be dead. You'll have five, angry knights gunning for you, along with a couple hundred witches, squires, and former-knights. Exactly how did you plan to get out of here with an entire town of magical kind on your tail?"

Ruith's lip twitched. Erwen held her hand steady, the blade still at Arthur's throat. The other priest-esses began whispering to each other, some turned their gaze toward the path away from the castle.

"So, here's what we're going to do," I continued. "You're going to trade me for him. You take me and my magic prisoner. But when you *off with my head,* that shield will likely drop and all those men and the people in the town will come after you. So, I suggest we walk out of here and you do the whole sacrificing thing once we're out of town. Deal?"

"No."

The growl didn't just come from Arthur. It came from each of the knights. Though I'm not sure if Geraint's voice was amongst the chorus. I couldn't see him. The voices of dissent weren't just male, they were feminine and adolescent and old.

My thoughts scattered and I couldn't think straight at the show of dissent at my sacrifice. I felt swaddled, rooted, supported. It was the most amazing experience of my life and I was grateful. I was also determined.

The truth is, I didn't want to die. But I'd already done it before. I'd been brought back and given a second life, and in a short time, I'd gotten everything I'd never dared to dream of. I got a family. I'd been surrounded by hot men who knew how to handle their swords. And best of all, if I had to go out, I'd go down as a bad ass, heroic martyr.

They would write poems about me. Loren the Great. It would be an epic poem because so many things rhymed with Loren. Actually, no. There weren't any good rhyming words for my name.

I didn't need magic to take down these women. I still had my sword in my bag, and unlike Thalia, I had no problems with violence. By the looks of the cluster of priestesses standing off to the side and inching away from the scene, it looked like only the two in front of me had a thirst for a witch's blood. They could be easy pickings if I got them to perp walk me out of town.

"Well, that's a really swell offer, Van Ass," said Erwen. "But I don't see why I can't just kill him now and take you with us."

Before I could open my mouth to offer a reason I didn't have, Erwen raised the spear. Then everything went into slow motion.

I saw the glint of the blade as it rose up towards the pale disk of the moon. I knew that if that blade came down it would not only end Arthur's life, it would completely ruin my selfless effigy.

I needed to act fast. But I didn't know what to do? I only had a second to make a plan.

I still had my magic. Maybe I could blast the spear out of Erwen's hand? But I didn't have much control over my magic and it might wind up slicing Arthur. That would not cast me in a heroic light.

I could whip out my sword and block Erwen's strike. But I had to cast that idea aside. I was fast with my weapon, but not that fast. She'd have the spear in Arthur's flesh by the time I pulled out my blade. That would leave me looking like a lame fool.

Maybe I could levitate again? I could turn my body toward Erwen and launch myself at her. True, the spear might then pierce me instead. But I had been prepared to take that eventuality by becoming her hostage.

It would be brave. It would be ballsy. It would be bold.

My mind made up, I turned my body towards Erwen. But she wasn't there. She was on the ground. With Merlin on top of her.

I stood, dumbfounded, trying to puzzle out what had just happened?

Had the previous villain of this story just cock-blocked my grand gesture?

Erwen rolled Merlin off her. Blood stained her robes and her empty hand. It was clear to see that it wasn't her blood. Merlin had taken the spear to his body for a second time, this time on the other side of his torso. By the speed at which his tunic darkened, I could tell it wasn't good.

But I didn't have time to feel sympathy for the devil. Erwen's hands were empty. The spear had rolled off to the side. Near Ruith.

Ruith's dark gaze caught mine. Evil glossed her lips as she sneered. It would be a race to see who could claim the weapon first.

Ruith and I moved at the same time. She was closer to the spear than I was. But I was faster. Unfortunately, not fast enough.

Ruith's fingers were nearly around the weapon. Before she could close her grasp, her body was yanked back. Her face did a comical transformation, morphing from triumph to confusion as she was jerked up into the air.

I snatched up the spear, but I couldn't perform a victory dance. Wrapped around Ruith's waist was what could only be described as a tentacle. The monstrous arm came from the moat. And it wasn't alone. Another tentacle reached out and ensnared Erwen's sandaled foot. It yanked her up into the air as well.

Erwen dangled upside down. The damn hypocrite wasn't wearing any underwear. But I had no time to feel any vindication. Screams broke out amongst the priestesses as they watched the display. I clutched the spear with one hand and reached for my sword with the other.

The women scattered, running full sprint for the path towards town. Sisterhood went in the air with Erwen and Ruith. It was every woman for herself.

The monstrous arms yanked Erwen and Ruith down into the moat. There was a gurgling sound as their bodies were submerged. The silence that followed was eerie.

"What the hell was that?" I finally managed.

"I went for backup, like you said."

I turned to the side to see Viviane propped up on the bank. She smiled proudly. She also had Erwen's sandal in her hand. But when she caught me looking at it, she hid it behind her back.

I twisted the hard-won weapons in my hand as I looked down at the water witch. Technically, Vivi's decision to go get help was my idea. So, the credit for the sea monster showing up in the nick of time should go to me. Which meant that I saved the day and should receive the cheering and, hopefully, knighting.

"Loren," Arthur shouted from behind me.

I turned to face him, prepping myself for some shoulder-hoisting. But Arthur's hands were otherwise occupied. He cradled Merlin's limp body in his arms.

"You need to get that shield down," he said. "We need to get him inside."

Behind Arthur, the townsfolk had gathered at the edge of my shield. They all pushed and prodded against the invisible wall. No one cheered. Many eyes were fixed on Merlin's lifeless body.

I'm certain the puzzlement showed on my face as I looked at the man who had started all of the drama, the man who had led his brother and the knights into a trap in Sarras, the man who had attempted to drain the life out of his wife.

Arthur's chin rose defiantly, his gray eyes reflected granite. "He's still family."

22

_____

"Where did you come up with such an idea?" said Gwin.

"A story I read," I said.

"Do you think it will work?" Vivi asked.

We sat at the bank on the side of the moat. Gwin and I had gotten Viviane out of her white nightgown and put her in a lavender shift dress that complimented her ghostly pale skin. Vivi had balked at the pastel and opted, instead, for a bright gold color that made her look like a jaundiced seahorse. But we let her and her bedraggled sense of fashion slide when the water witch couldn't stop smiling at herself in a hand mirror. And now she would complement the deathly outfit with blood-red shoes.

We all held a pair of Manolo Blahniks between us. The three of us chanted, funneling the magic of the ley line into the heeled slippers hoping to make a transformation.

The air heated around us, the atmosphere pulsing with power. We got the hint that the spell was fully baked when the shoes left our joined hands and began floating. Gwin reached up and captured the levitating shoes and then turned to the wide-eyed water witch.

"You ready, Viviane?" Gwin asked.

"My friends call me Vivi. You can call me that too, if you want."

"Are you ready, Vivi?" asked Gwin.

Vivi nodded her head enthusiastically. I almost wasn't certain if her excitement was for the shoes, the possibility of walking, or having another friend stand by her.

Vivi sat on the moat, but her feet dangled in the water. She took a deep breath as she lifted first one and then her other leg out of the stream. Gwin slipped a shoe on Vivi's right foot, while I slipped one on the left. Then together, we helped her come to standing.

It was like teaching someone how to ride a bike.

And Vivi started without the training wheels of flats. The Manolo's were five inches, but she insisted. Honestly, I would've too. They were killer shoes.

For the first twenty minutes, it was a comedy of errors as Vivi fell down, got up, wobbled her knees and windmilled her arms. But not once did she give up. And finally, she got the hang of it.

"I'm standing. I'm standing on my own two feet."

And then, of course, she fell down. But she made the choice to get back up and start again. And then again.

We left her on the drawbridge an hour later. She continued to practice walking in the magical shoes, determined to make it from one side of the bridge to the other without falling. It would likely take her all night.

"I was gonna go check on Morgan before dinner," I said. "You coming?"

"No, I'm going to check on Merlin."

Gwin's smile, which only moments ago had been filled with real happiness and joy, turned wary and defensive. Merlin was now in Morgan's sickbed in the infirmary. The second wound he'd sustained from the Spear of Destiny was a terminal one. There was nothing that could be done for him, except to keep him comfortable as he transitioned. Every day since he'd been brought inside, Gwin was his constant companion.

Many of the townsfolk had come to Merlin's bed to pay their respects. As I watched each victim offer compassion to the villain, I couldn't hide my contempt and confusion. It seemed the only people who stewed about this turn of events were me, Morgan, and Lance. So, in response to Gwin's announcement, I simply gave her hand a squeeze and headed in the opposite direction.

Peeking inside Morgan's bedroom, I saw the dark-haired woman lying in bed with her head bent over a thick text that sat in her covered lap. She turned a page with one hand and reached out with her other. Her gaze stayed fixed on the book as her fingers traced the lines of text. After a moment, her brow furrowed and she frowned.

She looked up and over at her outstretched hand. She looked at her empty palm in confusion, and then she looked at the nightstand. On the stand sat a glass of water. Morgan looked from her hand to the glass.

She shut the textbook. She flexed her hand. Her brow creased and her lips screwed in concentration.

She opened her hand again. The glass of water didn't budge.

Slowly, Morgan's empty hand lowered. Her eyes closed and she sighed.

My eyes stung with guilty tears. Thickness spread through the back of my throat, but another apology couldn't make its way out. I shifted my weight to turn out of the room when a floorboard creaked.

Morgan's eyes shot open. When she saw me, her face transformed from despair to delight. But the change was so forced it gave her whiplash and she slumped back against the headboard.

"Hey, Loren. I didn't see you there." Her bright smile reminded me of her sister's fake hostess smile. "I hear Viviane's taken her first few steps today."

I nodded, coming into the room. Just as I'd held my tongue with her sister, I decided not to broach the subject of Morgan's loss of power again. In this aspect, not speaking our truths, we were just like every other dysfunctional family out there.

"There's nothing like a great pair of shoes to transform a woman," I said, the same fake, bright smile on my face. "Just look at Cinderella. Or Elphaba."

"El-who?"

"You know; the Wicked Witch from *The Wizard of Oz.*"

"Oh. I never knew that was her name. Just the direction. But now, maybe we'll go see the Broadway play when I'm better. Since I'm not a witch anymore, Arthur has no reason to keep me here."

I tried to hold onto my smile, but I was out of practice with fake family gibberish. "Morgan, I'm so sorry."

But she shook her head. Her smile this time was less fake and more enthused. "Are you kidding? I got exactly what I wanted. I can go to college now. Not online, but a real college with dorms and fraternities and keggers."

She turned to look at the glass of water on her nightstand and shrugged.

"Honestly, living without magic will take some getting used to," she continued. "But if losing my power is what was necessary to get to my dreams, I'll take it. Please stop with the guilt trip, cuz. I'm over here drinking lemonade. Metaphorically."

She reached out and I came into her arms for a hug. She'd felt empty when we'd come back from the Tor. But now I felt a hum of life in her. That jolt made me believe her.

"Go on or you'll be late for dinner. I hear Igraine's making your favorite." She gagged and shuddered. Then she leaned over and reached for the glass of water and opened the text back up.

## 23

I headed down to the Great Hall. I could smell all manner of good medieval foods as I approached the doors. I also heard all manner of revelry inside.

Having been alone or with just one or two people most of my life, I had originally balked at the idea of existing in such a large tribe of noisy, overbearing, fiercely loyal, and unfailingly caring people. But I'd gotten over it.

My steps picked up to know what Igraine had mixed up in her pots. I'd planned to eat the main meal with the squires and talk medieval sports and their favorite picks for the next World Cup. When dessert came around, I planned to flit off to sit with Gwin and a few of the other witches my age, relatively speaking since everyone was at least fifty calendar years older than me. Then I'd head off to bed in my own room and rest, wake up, ride my magical horse, handle my squire duties, and do it all again.

This was home. A place I could be myself and not pretend. A place where I was welcome and no one made me feel like I didn't belong. Which was why my heart stopped and dropped like a stone in my gut when I opened the doors to the Great Hall and the room quieted with all eyes on me.

My hands went to my face, but I hadn't eaten anything. So, I couldn't have something in my teeth.

I patted my chest, but I was wearing a shirt and... yes, pants. And underwear too. So, I wasn't showing my ass.

I couldn't figure out what gave? Unless someone had realized I had borrowed Lady Mara's crown when we'd gone to lock the Spear of Destiny in the vault. But I was gonna put it back.

"Loren Van Alst, come forward."

My feet set a path towards Arthur without any conscious thought. As I walked forward, I noted that all the squires and knights were lined up in front of the great table where Arthur and his knights sat at each meal. Lance and Geraint stood on one side of an open path, while Tristan and Percival stood on another. As I came forward, each man drew his sword. My heart kicked at my chest cavity, wondering if I was about to be beheaded for playing princess with a borrowed crown.

But then I saw Gawain. He came to stand before Arthur, a sharp smile cut his handsome face. Those coffee-colored eyes twinkled with something that resembled pride as I drew near him.

"Will you kneel, my lady?" he asked.

I looked around the room. All the townsfolk stood. All wore smiles. There was an air of excitement zipping through the hall. This couldn't be that bad.

I took a deep breath, and a leap of faith. I kneeled before Gawain.

"My lords and ladies, I present to you Lady Loren Van Alst of the house of Galahad. She has proven herself in battle and, I believe, she is worthy of consideration of a seat at the high table of Camelot."

I felt my body tremble as the gravity of Gawain's words shook me. For the second time today, my eyes burned and my throat seized. It was all I could do to stay balanced on my knee.

"Who amongst the Knights will support this claim?" asked Gawain.

"I will," said Tristan, with a valiant nod of his blond head.

"I will," echoed Percy. A manic gleam shone in his eyes, but I saw dogmatism there as well.

"I will," said Lance. His voice was firm and sure.

Last up was Geraint. He gave me one, final assessing sweep. When his gaze locked on mine, I wasn't sure of my grade. Until he nodded his head. "I will."

I let out a gush of air, nearly toppling over. It was done. I had done it. I wanted to stand up and cheer, to throw my hands in the air and do a little dance. But I held still as Arthur came forward with the business end of a sword pointed at me.

"Do you swear to protect the weak and defenseless, to live by honor and for glory, to despise pecuniary reward, to fight for the welfare of all, and obey those placed in authority?"

That was a tall order. But like hell would I say no. "I will."

"Do you swear to guard the honor of fellow knights, to respect the honor of women, to eschew unfairness, meanness and deceit, to keep faith and speak truth at all times?"

Arthur raised an eyebrow. He was messing with me. But I knew these vows to be ones taken by every man here and every man that had come before these ones. This was the Knight's Code of Chivalry and I had to abide by it if I wanted the job.

"I will."

"Do you swear to persevere to the end in any enterprise begun, to never refuse a challenge from an equal, and to never turn the back upon a foe?"

"I will." That part, at least, was easy.

"Then by the power vested in me by my father, and his father before him, and his father before him, and by all the witnesses here, I dub thee Dame Galahad."

Arthur tapped me with the sword on both my shoulders.

"Arise, my lady."

He offered his hand and helped me up to the cheers of the entire town. I was embraced and clapped and, wait for it, hoisted up on the shoulders of Percy and Lance. Igraine stuffed me with all manner of garbage. Music played and I made a hack of medieval line dancing. I laughed and danced and stuffed myself until I couldn't see straight.

The party was still in full swing when Gawain tapped me on the shoulder. I'd been dancing with Yuric, Maurice, and a few other squires to a pop song from someone's cell phone plugged into speakers. I turned away from the boys and faced the man.

"Are you cutting in?" I asked.

"No," said Gawain. "I'm taking you away."

"Even better."

I left the squires and headed out of the hall with the knight. I knew that whole friend zone thing wouldn't last long. But as we headed out of the room, the other knights fell into step beside us. We all wound up in the Throne Room. My libido and its disappointment took a backseat when Gawain pulled out my grandfather's chair and waved a hand indicating that I should take a seat in it.

The seat fit my backside like a glove. It was warm, as though it had been waiting for me all along. I rested my back against its stiff wood and knew I'd found my place, my purpose.

"You were up with Morgan earlier?"

I looked up to find Arthur looking down at a stack of papers, but I was pretty sure he was addressing me as Morgan wasn't accepting many visitors.

"Yeah, yeah I did see her earlier."

"She's well?" Arthur's finger tapped the tops of the papers to put them in line. His gray gaze remained hooded.

A slow grin spread across my face at this evasive tactic. He was so busted. "You could go and see for yourself if you-"

He turned away from me and bellowed to Lance.

I leaned back in my chair. I was living in a live action, young adult novel without any vampires. At least I didn't think there were any vampires in real life.

"So, what's the new quest?" I asked, turning to my right. "Are we going after Templars? Maybe do some dragon slaying?"

"We don't slay dragons," said Percival, his tone offended. "They've been notoriously maligned throughout history when they're actually very gentle creatures."

I could only nod at his words as my brain tried to catch up and process. Dragons were real.

"We've received word that the Ring of Gyges has been spotted," said Arthur.

"Gyges?" I asked. "Why does that sound familiar?"

"There were stories written about it by Plato in his work *The Republic*," said Geraint. "About a king who stole a magical ring that would turn him invisible."

"Invisible or invincible," said Lance. "The translation is poor."

"*That* Ring of Gyges?" I said. "The one people believe Tolkien based *The Hobbit* off of? Wait, are hobbits real?"

"We believe the ring to be in the possession of this man." Arthur laid an 8x10 photograph on the table.

The moment the photographic paper hit the table a loud grumble went up through the room. All eyes went to me. I'd eaten a lot of food at my knighting ceremony, but not much more than usual. No, my stomach didn't grumble because of indigestion. It grumbled with boiling, roiling anger.

"Son of a...Spartan." Remembering my vows, I managed at the last second not to curse.

"Do you know this man?" asked Gawain.

"Yeah," I groaned. "He's my ex; Leonidas Baros."

I snatched the picture up and glared at the man who'd broken my heart not once, but twice. Even in the picture, it was clear to make out his large, muscular body that had been honed during his time fighting Persian invaders back in the 5th century. Those chiseled cheeks had softened under my touch. I knew the feel of the mass of curls framing those pale, pupil-less eyes.

"And he's no ordinary man," I said. "He's a Chosen."

"You mean a human in service to the Greek gods?"

Yup. The mark of a Chosen was the removal of their soul through their eyes, that's why they no longer had any eye coloring. But that wasn't the only thing extraordinary about Lenny.

"He's been in service to the Olympians since 480 B.C. when his Spartan army lost the Battle of Thermopylae."

"He's a Spartan?" asked Arthur.

"No. He's *the* Spartan. He's King Leonidas. You know; *This is Sparta!*" I quoted the popular action movie that depicted Lenny and his three-hundred soldiers during that fateful battle. Lenny and I never had a chance to get any closure after our last break up. "I call shot-gun because I'm going on this mission, right?"

<hr>

**Catch Loren on her first official quest in**
*The Ring of Gyges*
**Book Two in the Misadventures of Loren!**

# ALSO BY INES JOHNSON

Lover of fairytales, folklore, and mythology, Ines Johnson spends her days reimagining the stories of old in a modern world. She writes books where damsels cause the distress, princesses wield swords, and moms save the world.

You can sign up for her mailing list and receive alerts and free reads at http://bit.ly/InesReaders.

## The Nia Rivers Adventures

Dragon Bones

Demeter's Tablet

Templar Scrolls

Serpent Mound

Eden's Garden

## The Misadventures of Loren

Spear of Destiny

Ring of Gyges

Hammer of God

www.ingramcontent.com/pod-product-compliance
Lightning Source LLC
Chambersburg PA
CBHW071244190726
48292CB00007B/2407